Tide Running

ALSO BY OONYA KEMPADOO

Buxton Spice

OONYA KEMPADOO

Tide Running

PICADOR

First published 2001 by Picador
an imprint of Macmillan Publishers Ltd
25 Eccleston Place London SW1W 9NF
Basingstoke and Oxford
Associated companies throughout the world
www.macmillan.com

ISBN 0 330 48252 1

1 3 5 7 9 8 6 4 2

A CIP catalogue record for this book is available from
the British Library.

Typeset by Intype London Ltd
Printed and bound in Great Britain by
Mackays of Chatham plc, Chatham, Kent

Tide Running

Sea Breathing

The sea rolling and swelling up itself down by them rocks on Plymuth Point. Breathing out, sucking 'e belly back in. Every time it spuff slow, li'l crabs stop and hold on tight to the rocks. It fooling them. Only snorting and slurping back in, snuffling and bubbling. Them white crusty shells on the deep black rocks hissing and crackling every time the sea show 'e ribs. Big sea-eggs, urchins, tuck down in the holes and cracks. Some pack-up together so close, all you can see is a poison-black patch, long prickas sticking out 'gainst the green coral. Make you skin crawl. I stay still, still as the rock face behind me.

Out past the swellin' chest, all blue and green, the sea stretch 'e arm way up along the hills. Past Arnos Vale, Culloden, Moriah and Castara. Every time it heave, the arm ripple and, far far away, white waves wash over rocks, silent. Long white fingernails stretching out, clawing and scratching at the cliffs. The hills don't take-on the sea beating-up on they feet. Them hills stand the way they always was. Spirits in the valleys, smooth green humps and dark trees. The only thing that does change on them is the colours. They turning brown quick now. Every sky-clear day, blazing sun burning off more green. Soon will only be dry brown – and then fire. Real fire. Smoking and spreading with the breeze over them hills' shoulders. Burning for days. Leaving black scars. And then the sea go laugh. Shake-up 'eself and romp with the breeze. Show-off to the beat-up hills, booming 'gainst the cliffs and blowing out the biggest waves 'e can push. Then the sea go turn up 'e colours, swallow down the green, lighten the light blue and darken the deep. Liven up 'eself and laugh. Everything 'bout the sea big-up in them dry-season days, even the fish and all. Them days, the sea does talk more. Make me want it more. And when I walk down the hill from home, brown grass go crunch under me foot and the hot smell'a the land go dry-up me nose. Trees drop leaves like brown paper, seedpods crack open and rivers disappear. But the sea, 'e does get stronger. I like it for that. If there wasn' no sea, I must would feel lock-up. In a box with only the top open to the sky.

An' then, in the full'a the rain season, heavy rain does come and out the sea spirit. And the hills start living again, steaming, trees stretching out and bamboo bending with new leaves. The rain does bring-out every kind'a green you can imagine, everything dripping. I does say then, 'It look like the sea turn upside down' 'cause the sea turn same grey like the sky, green as the land, water beating down everywhere like if the sea upside-down 'eself in true. But even then, the land can't give you that sea feeling. And I know when I look at the sea, dark and flat so, that big fish breeding, things that I can't see going on down there. Deep in the belly of the sea. Is the same sea that does reach everywhere. When I look at the silva-line on the sea, it more far away than the skyline on the land. That's 'cause the sea so big. If I could'a never see it at all, nowhere round me, it go be like you lock me up. Drain something out'a me and leave a hole in me chest.

I breathe in and let it out in time with the next swell'a water under me. Two li'l sergeant fish, yellow and black stripe, pass over the black sea-egg prickas. I pull up me t-shirt onto me neckback and watch me shadow move 'cross the coral. Wave me fingers to see the extra waggles the water make with the shadow.

'E Rough Today

Ossi still sleeping. He always sleeping. All hours of the day sleeping he long lazy self. That's why he growing so, but I still taller than he. I step outside and early morning brace me with a strong salt breath. Sea rough today. White and frothy, churning. Breeze forcing 'eself all in me nose, me belly, waking up sleepy creases in me skin. Blow me pee sideways so it don't reach the drain, wipe it clean away.

Back inside. I pass through the bedroom to the closed-up kitchen. Pan on the stovetop still warm, bay leaves and water left in the bottom. Mudda just gone out for the day. She gone to meet the goods boat in Scarbro. Me sister Lynette and she Baby Keisha still sleeping in the other half'a the bedroom, behind the plywood. I put some more water in the bay leaves and boil it up. Can't find no green tea, no milk powder. Some bread in the bag hook-up on the wall. Unbolt the top of the kitchen door and the pushy breeze sweep the morning in. Past the hot tin cup in me hand and into the kitchen, brighting it up. Bright up the yellow counter that the wood ants eating out. Show up the brown lino mash into the concrete floor. But the kitchen clean, put-away. I finish the tea and make for the bedroom. Ossi still sprawl out. Mouth open, hand resting on he totee, bedsheet bunch up at the bottom of the bed. I bram the kitchen door on my way out. Stompy go be waiting for me by the jetty.

Road cool under me feet. Still chewing me bread slow, carrying me shirt on one shoulder. I clean out the yampy from me eyes, scrape inside me noseholes. Past Masta Barbar closed-up shop and Arnold Minimart. Past the junction, community centre, Bingey Rumshop, the school. All still closed-up. Reach the end'a the village by the Mystery Tombstone, turn down to the sea. Breeze quiet on this side. Fine-fine leaves on the big tamarind tree only trembling. Out past the point, white caps frisking and winking but in the bay by the jetty, the sea just lapsing. Little fishing boats rocking, dipping side to side. A yacht anchored and the big old trawler still there, the one the fella live on. Tide up. Only a small strip'a sand beach showing, rainbow colours moving on a engine-oil patch. Stompy at the end of the jetty fixing and loading, he big tough belly shakin' as he thump the gas container down in the boat.

'Yuh reach late,' he don't look up. 'I thought you wasn' coming again.'

I don't answer.

'Pass dat bucket, leh we go.' Stompy look up. 'Pass de bucket! Wha' happen to you, yuh still sleeping? Stan' up holding yuh crotch . . . as if you have anything to hold!'

I pass the bucket and suck the last bread out'a me teeth. Stompy still looking up at me from the boat. Bleach-end hair sticking up round he big face. Big flat nose flaresing, small piggy eyes bury down between he fleshy forehead and cheeks.

'Marnin',' I lean right over he face, bracing on my knees.

Piggy eyes lighter than he black skin looking right back at me.

'Marnin'! Marnin'! Is midday already, get yuh tail in

7

and leh we go!' He tug at the starter rope and I jump down in the boat, jerking Stompy to one side as the engine ketch.

'Wha' wrang wit' you dis mornin'?' He buff me but I laughing. I push us off from the jetty and spread myself out on the bow, fixing me balls, squinting out to the skyline as the boat swing round.

Is years now I fishing with Stompy. Since I small. He the one always come and call for me when I don't come out. Mudda always saying, 'Go, go! Look how much he tryin wit' you'. Stompy don't talk much. And he like the sea but he don't like going down in the water. He like to stay on top in the boat. And he look out'a place on land. Two fat laps at the top'a he thighs rubbing and smacking when he walk, two piece'a leather skin scraping together there. One'a he legs bigger than my waist. Slim he call me. Slim and Slims – me and Ossi.

I watch him as we motor out of the bay. Me going backwards, he forward, sitting by the engine. Belly forcing he legs to cock-open. Tight little tiger-pattern trunks peeking out from under. These trunks is he old ones, faded so you can hardly see the stripes. He have a new black pair he does wear when he taking tourist to fish. Specially woman tourist. I never gone with him then. He acting now like he don't know I watching him. He big shape weighing down the boat at the end, like it always been there, taking me out to deep sea. A warm flash inside me. Warm as the sun now heating up the day, flashing on the water. Great tot-tots shuddersing on top he belly as we start hitting the small swells. A bullneck join he head to he shoulders. Round shoulders slope down to arm, down to reach the throttle. Other arm always resting on he thigh, hand dangling down on the inside. A big black turtle sitting there, driving me out in this li'l yellow shell, bright against wavy blue. Behind him the flat sand-line, a green band'a hills behind grey coconut-trunk matchsticks, then the smooth morning-blue sky. Bright colour pirogues all round the jetty tippling like floating insects, bowed bamboo fishing-poles like whiskers dipping. They all listening to the lonesome zinc roof at the end'a the jetty preaching down to them. Swarmed to the lights in the night, then morning ketch them still scatter round the jetty-end, tipping and listening to the preacher roof over the old diesel pumps. Pelicans and gulls does come and join the congregation, stirring them up, diving into the sea and clapping they wings when the roof sing out. On a afternoon, boys'd be jumping off the jetty, splashing and whooping back at the roof while the boats watch on.

We right out of the bay now and the swells big and hissing. From down in the troughs, land disappearing. Stompy still looking ahead. Turtle and the engine ploughing on. Every time the bow shoot up in the air and crash down, my whole body lift up and thump back down. I bouncing and thumping, legs flapping up. Stompy grinning, still not looking at me, making sure my arse getting wet.

''E rough today!' I shouting.

He straighten he face and half nod.

Heading out towards Pigeon Point side, the hills dark and far away now. Is only deep-deep blue around. Rolling and frisking us up. I start baiting the lines. Stompy slow down the engine and I tie the jiggly green and orange rubber squids on. I throw one line in and give him the roll. Fix up the other line and pitch it out. Bonitos start biting at a rate. One time, Stompy start hauling in. I can see flashings out'a the white water in the wake. Silver flashing fighting hard. Stompy pulling in easy, slow. Another one bite, jerking the line back out'a his hand. He look at me grinning and haul in faster.

* * *

She go be waking up just now, Baby Keisha. Scrambling over Lynette and sliding on she belly to the edge of the bed. She does always grip two handfuls of bedsheet to lower sheself down. Plop down on the floor. I watched she yesterday again, poking about under the bed while Lynette still sleeping. Pulling the wash pans full'a clothes, the big white bucket with a strong tight cover. Pushing she head forward to get a better look, crawling into the dark to the suitcase and tugging at the buckle. Soon as she hear Lynette voice, she hustling out, scrabbling to meet her mother's face hanging upside down over the edge of the bed.

In our house, Baby Keisha is the everyday smile'a we lives. When we all watching TV, is Keisha that does make us feel like a family. She make us have something that is ours, we own flesh and blood. Lynette child, the same one Mudda beat her for getting pregnant with. She like to romp with Ossi. He know how to make she squeal and churgle till Lynette have to tell him, 'Stop! You go give the child short breath'. But she like me better. I have a way with she, like something, Lynette don't know what. Keisha quiet with me. Climb up on me lap, sit on top me head with no fear when I carry she about. Tight neat li'l body, shiny li'l fingers and toes, reach out to me whenever I home. Almost like I is she father. Lynette does watch, she don't know what to feel. Sometimes the way Keisha stick onto me when I leaving, crying when I don't take her, I know Lynette wondering how it would be if she was to live in a house with she baby father, just the two'a them and Keisha. Like that family in *Days of Our Lives*, he going out to work and she staying home with they lovely rosy baby. He kissing them at the doorway and waving goodbye every morning. Lynette feel bad that Keisha only have her. Make her feel like less of a mother, specially when she slap her and Keisha run to me. Still, is her pride and joy. And Keisha, the smallest thing in the house, know how to bring out the best from each'a we. She know how to play she granny for a mint, Ossi for a tickle, me for a cuddle and Lynette for all the rest she need.

* * *

Them fish giving us a fight this morning. About a dozen bonitos bouncing in the bottom of the boat already. All my arms aching, my knees and shins bungered and bruise up – and it's early still. Stompy like it so, when the sea getting on, not giving you an ease. It does raise up something inside him. Make him look different: wild-up and ready for anything. Is the only time he eyes shine and he laughing good, not just skin-teeth, real laugh. Pulling in the line, working the engine, checking the waves, all the time we rolling over them, near sideways. He could'a have four hands and a spare set'a eyes. He can stand up, sit down, turn round while he doing all that and not get knock down or grab onto the side.

'Whey we going now?'

He start heading out deeper.

'Tuna!'

I can rest now. Pull in my line. He standing up guiding the boat through the pitching. Keep going, quite out, the white line of the reef far back. Tobago nearly gone now, just blue hills with black cloud shadows.

'Ha-haai! De buggas can't get away today!' He roaring.

Slow down the engine, lean forward and grab one of the smaller bonitos. It jerking and flapping in his hand before he gut it open. Bait he line with pieces, throwing the guts into the water, smiling like he know what he feeding down there.

Ketching a set'a kingfish today. He hauling them in, rolling about playing with them curving and arcing out the water, bawling, 'Whoa, yuh bugga!' Bottom lip glinting like the sea water drops on he black skin.

'Yuh like dat, eh?'

'Hunfh.'

He lean over and heave a big fish into the boat, scraping the fat stiff side on the edge and then let it slide down head first into the pile'a small fish. Set them off flopping again.

'Heh-hey!' He slap the smooth skin of his last fish hard and we heading in to the reef.

* * *

When I reach home, Ossi still in bed, Baby Keisha after him. 'Os-si! Os-si!'

'Uhmn,' Ossi close he gaping mouth and suck in some dribble without opening he eyes.

Keisha bright li'l eyes just above the bed, reach up and slap a arm down on the mattress, hard as she could.

'Os-si! 'Ake up!' Stamp and slap again.

Ossi roll he head and she grip the edge'a the bed excited. Nuthing happen. She bram the bed with both arms, hardly making the sponge bounce, tiptoesing to reach. She stay like that, stretch up on she toes and look down at them. Ossi open one eye and spot the top'a she fuzzy head.

'Raagh!'

He lunge over and grab she hands, setting off shrieks full blast. He let go and pretend to sleep again, she gurgle and gee, ready to slap at the bed again, eyes and li'l front teeth shining.

Lynette knocking round in the kitchen. Listening to Ossi raaghing and Keisha squealing was one of her morning pleasures. Ossi stand up in the kitchen doorway and Keisha butt she head through he legs.

'Whey Mudda?'

'I ain' know,' Lynette answer and go into her room.

Hear her dragging the clothes basin out from under she bed, back door banging open, and the basin drop outside. Then the empty metal squeak'a the standpipe. But no sound of water. She steups loud and come back in, big comb stick in she hair.

'Ossi, you go have to fetch some wata fuh me. No wata in de pipe.'

Plunk sheself down on the straight-back chair by the table.

Ossi don't answer. Stand rubbing from the back'a he head to the front, leaning on the doorpost gazing out across the dirt yard to the sea crashing on the rocks.

I rest me sea-beat self on the bed and watch Lynette undoing she plaits. She keeping a eye on Ossi long back in the doorway, Keisha mash cooling and the steam rising out'a the pan on the stovetop.

'Yuh hear me? I have to wash today.'

'Oh God, I hear you. I ain' even eat nuthing yet, drink nuthing yet, and you want me fetch wata?'

Hand drop from he head and he turn looking for the bread.

'What washing yuh talkin' 'bout when it have no wata in de pipe!'

'You still have to fetch some wata fuh me to cook.'

The pan boiling now, shaking and rattling. Lynette eye on Baby Keisha trying to back down the outside steps.

'Come here! Ossi, ketch her.'

He lift her by one arm and plop she on the kitchen floor. She start churgling again and patter back to the steps.

'Come here gyal!' Rumble through a mouth full'a bread and he grand-charge her, stamping he feet.

She squeal loud as she can and stick one foot out in the air behind her. Lynette finish plaiting the hair she had loose out and combed, stick the comb back in she plaits and get up.

Time pass like every day in Plymuth. Ossi fetch two bucket'a water from the standpipe down the hill, enough for Lynette to bathe Keisha and cook. Jump on he bike and gone for the day. She watch him curling heself onto the small bike wearing nuthing but the same shorts he was sleeping in. Gone. Off roaming. Hanging around them big fellas by Masta Barbar shop. Looking to trouble people girl-chi'ren, even though he is a child heself. One long aimless child.

Lynette can't wash clothes now. Maybe the water might come back on later. She go cook something from what provisions it have in the house, straighten the gallery, sweep the front porch and yard, finish she own hair, Keisha hair, feed her and try to make her sleep. Before *Days of Our Lives* start at two o'clock.

Me an' Ossi

'Ossi, dem people pass in Plymuth today?'

'Na. I ain' see dem.'

Watching TV on a afternoon.

'Dey ain' come for de whole week.'

'Un-unh, dey was here de otha day.'

'When?'

'You was out fishin'.'

'Dey came in de daytime?'

'Un-huh. Dey went out by de rocks.'

'Whea boy, you ain' even tell me nuthing.'

'Shu' you mouth nuh. An' move yuh foot, you barring de TV.'

Me eyes rest on Ossi. He lean forward, both palms down on the settee next to him, long neck stretch out, mouth henging open.

'Haa boy. Dat fella real stupid, yuh-know. Watch he. Eh.'

Juk he chin at the TV without looking at me.

'He so stupid he don' see de woman horning he. Watch nuh!'

I watch the nice-face girl talking to Ridge. Them TV people look like they ain' real. Even though they is white people, they different from them white people I see here. And some'a these ones even come from America. Sound like the TV ones but they don't look like them. The TV ones, they skin smooth-smooth and white. It ain' red and shaky like them tourist girl. When you see some fresh tourist who just reach here, they skin white, it blinding you eye in the sun, but they looking sicky. Maybe is the plane does make them look so, flying all them hours, lock-up tight. Then when they on the beach, vendors does braid them tourist-lady hair. They set there for a whole hour or more taking the pain while the vendor plaiting tight, they forehead and ears red, paying big US dollars. It does make them look so ratty, when white people do they hair like that. All they white scalp showing and beads pink like they skin 'ttached to the end'a stringy plaits. The braids look don't take them but is so they like it. Specially when they ready to go back home – at the airport, li'l white girl-chi'ren keep spinning round flicking they head so you can hear the beads clicking. And they ain' dressing up to go on the plane – same old sandals and short pants but showing off the noisy beads, pink skin and white eyebrows.

'Watch eh. Watch eh. She go tell he dat is he baby . . . aye boy!' Ossi slap the settee hard with both hands, almost dribbling, laughing, cause he so right.

'Da fella real stupid boy!'

The big-city *Bold and Beautiful* music twang out before the KFC ad come on. We watch.

'Finga-lickin'!' Ossi rubbing he belly under his shirt. 'I could eat a piece'a dat now!'

'Dem brown-skin people is from Trinidad, yuh-know.'

'Na.'

'Yeah boy. Dem is Trinis. Watch it again next time, you go see. Dat is a KFC in Trinidad.'

A Mutual Life ad on now.

'Some'a dem Trinis does look like black people from foreign.'

'Yeah boy.'

A Trini-red man lift up he daughter into the air outside they picture-nice house. He Indian wife and grey-hair parents all looking up, smiling at the li'l girl. She have on socks and sandals and all'a they teeth milky white, healthy-looking and happy. The house have a driveway with a garage and a new car park-up like in them flims. Is true, when them Trinis come over to Tobago, they look like they come from foreign. Even when they ain' wearing all the Ray Ban and beach wrap and sporting Carib Beer towel, something does make them look like foreign. The skin look like it don't get much sun. Air-condition skin with darky knees and elbows – even the black-black Trinis. Is something 'bout the hairstyle or the way they walking and smelling'a suntan cream. A black Trini man come on holiday in Crown Point could'a be a black man just land from England – new short pants, new Reef sandals, walking puff-up, proud to be bareback. You can see they ain' 'custom. Toes softy like they never get air neither.

Bold and Beautiful starting again.

'Wha' Lynette cook?'

'Some rice an' somet'ing.'

Mudda foot start trudging up the front steps. The porch gate shake the whole house when she shove it shut and brace in the doorway. Plunk sheself down in she chair by the door.

'Whoy. Eh.'

Swipe off she back-to-front cap.

'Mammay, yuh bring Kentucky?' Ossi akse, he ain' even look round at she.

'Wha' de fuck you t'ink it is, boy! Yuh t'ink I scrunting me arse in town all day to bring fucking Kentucky fuh you?'

Steups. Slap she knee with the cap and swing she chin round, neck stretch out.

I shame for Ossi. He don't even see how red she eye is from the sun.

'Yeah boy, da' is junk food nuh. Ossi like all dat ole chicken fry up in ole oil.' I shove out'a the chair and go in the kitchen for me food. 'And he eat a'ready!'

Ossi don't look round from the TV.

*   *   *

Dem people does come driving into Plymuth. Is over three years now they coming here, for holiday in Tobago. First they uses to come with a short fat black fella, sometimes with a white smiley fella and they always goes straight to the jetty. I don't know what it is the jetty have for dem people, boy. They just come and set down on the jetty and watch the water. They don't swim. Nuthing. They have a son and a time I see he trying to fish. Sometimes he does swim but mostly they sit and drink from a drinks bottle. Just looking. Must be fish they looking for. Sometimes they get up from one side'a the jetty and follow them small fish, 'cross to the next side. They points at the pelicans diving. Or when a big fish jump they get all excitable and crane to see more. Sometimes they just watch we swimming and fooling 'round. Me and the lady eye always making four.

Dem people is from foreign. De lady is a mix-blood, look like she from Trinidad but a time I hear she call out to the boy and she don't sound Trini. The mister is a white fella and he tall. Yeah boy, the fella real tall. The small boy mix with the both of them but he take more from he mudda side. I does always watch out for when dem people drive through Plymuth. They uses to come twice a year, but now they coming to Plymuth regular, like they living here. When you see dem people driving in they car, it looking nice, boy. The car driving smooth-smooth. It ain' making no sound. And it have glass all around, window in the roof and all. Yeah boy. That car looking so sweet eh. Just like de lady. Sweet face, curly hair and catchy eyes. And she always wearing a white clothes. White take she complexion too, she dark and smooth skin. Both'a them slim and she tall too. You can't tell how old she is, the way how she walk kang-a-lang flapping she big foot so, or running race with the li'l boy on the jetty. Neither the mister, but he is a oldie-youngie. Looks young-young sometimes, and old other times. He have a big gluga-pipe sticking out on he neck and a big biscuit chest for such a slim fella. When he lie down on the jetty you only seeing toes, gluga-pipe and chin pointing up. He have flicky yellow hair and blue eyes with a funny-looking spectacles.

Dem people does sit on that jetty and talks to one another all the time. I don't know what it is they have to talk about so much. One day they come about four-thirty and talks till six-thirty. They come the next day too, same thing, talk till the sun gone down. Laughing sometimes in between, the lady long hands flying about. The next day, same thing. Three days running I see dem people talking. Them good for theyself, good for each another. The boy looking for crabs by the shore, trying to catch sea cocka-roach for bait, running back showing them, pushing it up in they face. He happy with heself too. Them is people, boy. I does watch them.

*　*　*

Since me and Ossi was small and uses to have shoot-off races in the bush by Rockly Bay, Ossi cock always bigger. He the youngest out'a all the boys but he could shoot the far'est. Almost like it surprise him. Open he eye big and hoot and run around braying afterwards, slapping me on me back like I is he li'l brother. A year younger than me and always next to me. Like a shadow, 'cept shadows don't talk. He loudmouth. He the one like to talk big and ballsy. Maybe 'cause he have that big thing in he pants that he always squeezing. People say we could'a been twins. I just smile when they say that 'cause I know that the things in Ossi mind is not in mine.

He like them girl's pem-pem. Big woman pum-pum too. I was ten, Ossi was nine, when we ketch it for the first time – a piece'a t'ing from them small girls. He was the one who went and call the girl down to the beach for me, so he had to get it too. Up to now he like sexing so much I does have to cuff him off the bed when he carrying on, dreaming and making noise and rubbing-up heself. Or if he hand fall on my totee, he rubbing that too. He go from girlfriend, same age as he, to big woman, some old as Lynette, one woman reaching near Mudda age. Only laughing after and telling me everything. He like to talk.

He have a way he does play li'l boy when he between them women. Aksing so-and-so to plait he hair and falling asleep with he head in they laps. Fetching water for them, then rubbing he back and saying how it hurting while he know the woman looking at he bumsey peeking out the top'a he pants. Watching the woman with he big round eye and thick long eyelash. Ossi know what he doing when it come to woman. Just the way he scratching he head and squeezing he cock like he don't know what to do with it, does make them girls laugh and touch him,

tease him with they big bubbies. He like all'a that. He tell
them women with big tot-tots that he like milk. 'Breast is
best'. They laugh and slap he bumsey. 'Boy go look fuh
yuh mudda!' He shouting back, 'But me mudda milk done!
I suck it dry'. They laughing but they watching he pants,
he pink wet bottom lip he always sucking, and he big
hands hanging. He does grow long nails on he left hand.
Them girls does put Cutex on them when they playing in
he hair. He can copy a she-voice and make everybody
laugh, cook in the kitchen with Lynette, help she wash
clothes and all them kind'a things, and still ketch pum-
pum.

Ossi always look out for me though. He never stop
trying to fix-up a t'ing for me. 'De girl dem like you. Is
me dem ah talk to, but is you dem want.' Even though
I tell him how many hundred times I don't like thick
bulupsie girl with big bubbie, he say that is my problem.
'If is slim virgin you want, look, Charlene daughter like
you.' But he don't understand, I believe in love, like in the
song. Spread my wings and fly away, think about it every
night and day. Me, I have to be free. Anyway, all the girls
them want the same thing – juk, juk, juk. And then they
want something else – a chain, a earsring, piece'a chicken,
softdrink. Dem say all that she want is another baby, she
got to have it. Is true. Is to tie you up, make you old
before you time. Make you a man but wort'less, just like
you father.

*　　*　　*

Most'a the time, me and Ossi spends riding them two
small bikes Mudda did give us for Christmas, five years'a
back. We fix-up them and ride. Raise-up the handlebars

and ride. Long-out the seat and ride. That's what we does all day. All the streets and the corners in Plymuth is like the veins on the back'a we hands. The main roads from Buccoo to Arnos Vale is them long veins running up we vibrating arms. The Shirvan Road and Soloman Hoychoy Highway is the big pumping thigh veins. And from Canaan to Crown Point and all them backstreets is blood veins running from we calves, spread out on we foot-tops. We can make them roads sing even with them li'l bikes. Is the next nicest feeling 'part from the sea feeling. A flying speeding freedom coming down Mount Irvine hill. Along the flat Turtle Beach road, orange six-o'clock sun and black bush shadows striping, flashing on us. Curving round the bendy Arnos Vale road, riding in the middle, ears cocked for the sound of a car. Stopping in the cool river-bed part. The part that always green even in dry season, where bamboo touching overhead and mango trees and sago palms marching up the driveway to the big house on the hill.

It don't matter what you wearing when you riding just for the feeling. We just be eyes, ears and legs, and bare blazing backs, it don't matter. Once you keep moving, cruising, back-pedalling, hands swinging – we rolling. We on a roll. Like them gulls. Wheel and turn. Far and high as them black seabirds. Sailing, circle round. Nuthing don't stop us till we done.

On a Sunday or a Saturday afternoon is different. Then I put on me blue and white meshy Nike shirt, white visor, blue and white bandanna tie round me neck and blue peepers. Ossi don't have no peepers, he say they hurt he eyes. He have no visor either, just a red bandanna and a maroon and white football shirt. I look the coolest. And the peepers gimme a protection. It have a mirror on the front so nobody can see me eyes. Unless I peep over the top. That is stylin'. A man must have a mystery 'bout him.

We only cruising on them dress-up times. No sweat. Slowly down the road, loopsing past people you want to notice you. Past the girls liming by the school gate. Pacing with the boys walking up and down. Stance by the dominoes slamming in front Bingey Rumshop. Drag you shoe, stop cool by the corner fellas. Who don't have bikes does be stepping in style. All the while them big Plymuth women does be sit down checking what really going on. Talking people name.

We hardly never rides into Scarbro. The road over the hills make you burn-out and sweaty by the time you reach there. And then them fellas in town have no mercy. Old bikes can't cut no style there. Laughing at how we hunch up on them li'l bikes, them fellas can make you feel small. A fella take away Ossi bike once and make pappyshow, fool around, in front'a everybody, till he ride in a pothole and bend the back wheel. We had to take turns pushing all the way back to Plymuth. Dem people pass us that time on the road. They wave to we.

Tomo and de Fellas

We pull up in front Masta Barbar. Tomo and de fellas liming outside. Masta Barbar is family to we. He does give we cuts for free but Ossi say he growing he hair. Right now he have it in corn-row plaits. I push my head in the doorway'a barbar shop, Charlo taking a cut. Is only room for two inside that teeny box. The fella who does do art works, had paint-up the outside. He paint a woman head with long hair and a man head with a airport stylin' – flat on top. And then he write underneath, 'Unisex Saloon, Masta Barbar' in red and blue curly writing. But I never see any woman set down in that barbar chair. Inside the shop it mark up 'No greasy hair'.

Charlo getting a all-in-one.

'Turn yuh head, let me see yuh head-back,' barbar say to me.

I turn me head round, still holding onto the doorway, so he could inspec' his work.

'It growing out.'

I swipe my hand on the 'Nike' he shave on me head-back just four days ago. 'Yeah boy. Quick eh?'

'Is dat little bit a coolie blood yuh have in you make yuh hair grow so fast.'

I roll some'a me twists while I watch barbar with he electric shaver. He running it over Charlo scalp, pressing hard. Skin raise-up in a ripple running in front the metal teeth. Ossi brace-up on the low mango tree by them fellas, listening.

'Where Lynette? I ain' see she pass today,' barbar akse.

'I ain' know. We leave home since morning.'

He always aksing after Lynette. Though we is family, I see the way he does watch her when she passing, and the way she call out to he. Sometimes I wonder if Baby Keisha is he child. Can't see no semblance though. She li'l face smiley and round, forehead bump-out and smooth. Barbar face serious and flat. For all the shaving and cutting he cut, he heself have a thick long beard.

A old electric fan hook up in the corner and some glass louvres open on the side where he have the speaker boxes. But when the breeze and all hot, and afternoon sun blazing in up to your waist, in there is a blistering hell that you have to suffer if you want a cut.

He finish skinning Charlo head with the shaver comb, leaving just a gristle'a hair, and now he take up the bare double-edge Gillette from the ledge and wipe it on he rag. Set about scraping and cleaning from one ear 'cross and up along Charlo forehead to the next side. Hold his head and twist it how he want it, grip it there, while his fingers scrunching into he palm. Hiding the little bendy blade. Only the skin-crawling scrape and Charlo freeze-up make you know it's there.

Tomo grater voice come out rough from the shade of the mango tree, 'Dat fucking police t'ink he smart, bu' he is a lickle boy. He aksing me, "Wha' you was doing las' night?" I tell he I was doing he mudda!'

The fellas round him set off laughing. Ossi skinning he teeth and rubbing he head.

'He ain' know me nuh. I is boss when it come to fucking police. I could cuss dem up an' down and dey could never arres' me fuh foul language. He just come out on de scene, an' playing big man!'

'Dey ketch Short Man de otha night in Scarbro,' Tiny put in. Tiny just start working for Tomo.

''Cause he too damn stupid. Everybody know dat you can't do no business in front de port when Sergeant John working there. All de rest'a dem big offica know me but dat one like to play hoity-toity. He like to play like he working fuh Scotland Yard. Every Tom, Dick an' Harry know dat. And Short Man don' know! He go always end-up in jail. He might as well tek-up residence in dat town house, he so stupid.'

Tiny shift he bony arse on the stone he sitting on, push at some loose gravel with he foot. Inside barbar shop, Charlo still freeze-up. The inching blade reach he other temple.

Tomo and he fellas always on the block. If they ain' outside Masta Barbar, they across by the junction, or outside Bingey Rumshop. Not a thing don't go on in Plymuth they don't know 'bout. Every one a'them fellas been in the town house some time or the other, but not for long. Tomo heself does go in every couple'a year for a week or so. Them fellas round him today is the ones selling weed mostly. The ones who selling crack don't come out so much in the daytime. Them is jumbies. Coming out in the night, silent with they eyes open big, hair natty and wild. In daylight, they look magger and dry-up, boo-boo still in they eye-corners, mouth black and tight and when they open it, stink breath knock you down. Lynette always saying them jumbies is the blight'a Plymuth and if me an' Ossi don't watch out, we go end up just like them – haunted for the rest'a we life. Lynette always the one harassing Mudda 'bout how useless we is, 'bout how long we out roaming the whole'a Tobago on them bikes. And that all we looking for is trouble. Mudda tell we to stay in the house and watch TV, but Lynette saying that if we don't find trouble, trouble go find we. Specially me. She does be on my case like a pest. Always checking, suspec'ing, looking right in me eye and warning. When I was small she was the one used to beat me.

Ossi up in the tree now, loop on like a Makajuel snake, watching Tomo close-up. Tomo is a thick-skin fella. Short, but nobody call him Shortie. From the back he look like a warty brown frog, round with small hands sticking out away from he body and two small feet with pointy toes in brown plastic slippers. Like a crapaud from the front too, shorts waist under he pop-out belly. When he laugh, you see spacey teeth, green and red jewels set in the front ones. He lips curl out showing all the gums, even the bottom ones, and he deep grater laugh does scrape out slow. He is not the big man though. The boss man does check him sometimes, cruising slow through Plymuth in a black car with tinting glass, arm hanging out the window down to the ground with a big gold wristband on it. In the dark'a the car, all you can see is the shine from the set'a gold chains sitting round he neck and a flash of he peepers, a woman eyes glitter from next to him. Boom-bass speakers pounding round the corner before you see his car. And he come to stop a little ways down the road. Tomo hustle round to the window and smile he crapaud smile. I never see the boss man step out'a he car. Only the long arm drapsed outside. He move it lazy so, when he talking to Tomo, the big hand turning belly-up like a fish, flopping back down. Them fellas say he have a gun. But he never shoot it. He never need to, 'cause the way he carry heself in that car will cool-off anybody head before they trouble he. So nobody don't.

Tomo gofer is a fella called Dobermann. Wherever you see Tomo, you see he. Not 'cause Tomo need protection or something so, but because Dobermann like to move like how he see on TV with them gangs, and real big-city blocks and alleyways, and police cars chasing you. Dobermann can make you forget that is hours sometimes before you see a car pass down Plymuth road, and even then, is only the mechanix fella in he bright pink Mazda. Dobermann serious and he only worries is how to stay cool when he bathing by the roadside standpipe. He never see them do that on TV so he only bathing in the night. When them fellas decide to take a sea-bath to pass time, Dobermann worries is how to do that with a cool stylin'. How to ease in the water and still look guardie. If you ever see a Dobermann swim, that is how he does look in the water – neck sticking up uncomfortable. But at night he look best. He long snout smelling the air round Tomo, small eyes seeing more than everybody own, tight slick body, head and neck stiff. He look like the real thing. Could'a be from one a'them gangsta-rap video. One night he even try yanking, talking like a Yankee – 'how youall go-eng bro' – but them fellas just watch he and laugh. Akse he if he wake-up proper yet.

Charlo peel heself off'a barbar chair and step outside rubbing he head-top. The fellas and Ossi turn to watch him.

'Eh boy, why you didn' take a shine an' done!'

Charlo just steups, shaking out he shirt and stamping. Close-up to him, I can see the skin on he neckback raw-looking from the sting of barbar mentholated spirits.

'I going an' tek a rest fellas.' Charlo start off down the empty road.

'Aye, Charlo, you 'ave cigritte?' Tiny shout.

He don't answer. He must'e see that nuthing wasn' going to happen this afternoon or later this evening. Nuthing go change. The fellas go be there talking the same shit-talk tomorrow and the day after. Budups might pass with the old car he fix up with mag rims and speakers, park-up and blast dancehall music for a while. Them girls go pass and gallery theyself. But nuthing new. Nuthing much doing. Ossi pull in he bottom lip, unloop heself from the tree and we pick up we bikes.

'I gone,' I tell Masta Barbar.

But wasn' nowhere to go.

Baywatch *and de Preacher*

Baywatch now showing, and is this night the soca-baptist preacher decide to preach. Park heself on the road corner by the Evertons' house, but we can still hear he speaker-funnel hailing clear over the TV.

And people, how are you tonight? preach out.

'Why dat damn man have to be tormenting people so?' Lynette set sheself with a cup'a cocoa-tea to watch the show, comb and curlers stick-up in she hair.

'You 'ave any more tea in de kitchen?' Ossi akse.

'Go see for yuhself nuh.'

The lifeguards and bouncy girls start smoothing on with the music. Big bare-chest muscly fellas with dark-shades, wet hair and slick smiles.

Was it a good day? Did you praise the Lord today? Or was it frauth with worry an' frustrashun?

The girls in they high-cut bath-suits, bubbies squeezing out shiny and stiff-looking. Ossi hand me a cup'a the thick spicy cocoa-tea.

Aren't ALL your days full of fatigue and woa?

'Why dat man don' rest he tail!' Lynette grumble. 'He is de one giving people frustrashun. Huh.'

Island of Romance. Gulls clacking round, speedboats cruising, chicks and guys playing netball on the beach. Ceejay, one of the specially bubbilicious girls, mincing over to talk to Mitch, face set up like she going to kiss him or take off she bath-suit or something, but is only 'Hi' come out she mouth.

People of Plymuth, when are you going to come to your SENSES? Every DAY dat's passing is precious! Gaad didn' take he best heffort, take he good good time and make you, for you to stay here WANDARING! LOST!

A ad about if you want love, call 1 800 psychic. Ceejay and Stephanie on they speedboat, just the two'a them, driving and smiling into the breeze. They flexy hair spinning out behind them like horse tail and they talking through they nose. Ceejay bend over, bam-bam up, bubbies down, sparky water skimming behind she.

'Da' one nice, eh?' Ossi slide down more on he seat.

Lynette cast she eye on he and steups.

Where are you going? What are you doing with your life? When Judgement Day come, where will you BE? With the sheeps or the goats?

Just so, the girls spy a boat ketching a'fire, the people on it jumping overboard. The girls' eyebrows serious-up, eyes come concern, pointing they arms, ready to rescue. 'Coastguard! Coastguard! Come in. Come in!' Speeding up, the people in the water bawling. Coastguard big boat coming.

'Dat is one t'ing I like da' place for, boy . . .'

Fire hose spraying, the girls done jump in the water already, saving them people but a body gone down. Stephanie diving down and coming up. Again and again, can't find the person. A coastguard fella, with all he tubes and t'ing, dive down. Pull up the sinking girl, she yellow hair moving like squid foot.

'She ain' dead nuh . . . dat is one t'ing I like foreign for, dem always have all de 'quipment for any kind'a 'mergency, boy.'

31

Ossi like to talk when he watching TV. Mouth always running. 'Watch nuh, dey go do dat t'ing 'pon de girl . . .' The coastguards and Stephanie pulling the drownding girl up into they boat. Even though she half dead, she toes pose-off pointing, bath-suit and lipstick fix-up perfect. '. . . Wha' dey call it, nuh. Dey go suck she mouth and press down on she chest. Eh. Dem lifeguard and dem does always do dat. She go wake up.'

The girl cough, sit up and smile. The rest'a the coastguards clapping. 'Yeah!'

Ads for Tums – now the man can eat a next cheeseburger. Sweet-talker Betty Crocker. Now Ceejay and Stephanie sitting on some rocks talking through they nose again. Rocks looking just like Plymuth Rocks, same gulls squalling, same kind'a sea slapsing.

And where are your chi'ren? LOST! You lost yuh chi'ren! You say is de TV take dem. De rumshop, de DRUGS! Lost, Plymuth people. Wandaring. And only YOU, only you O Lord, can help yuhself. Amen-ah. But de Devil, ohh, he have plans-ah . . .

I see Lynette ain' really watching the TV. Them girls taking pictures of one another. Running round on the sand and posing like them magazine girls. Pushing they bubbies together, pulling up one knee so. They gallery theyself.

Ossi grinning and twisting he head when they bend down. 'Oh gawd, boy. Uh!'

They putting on they gears to go and dive. A ad for Pepsid come on.

'Dem Amerrycan can real eat plenty, boy.' He watching the man eating pizza, mouth henging.

Look around you-ah! Not even school can save yuh chi'ren. CHI'REN MAKING CHI'REN! Young girls wearing skirt split up to they waist. KARNAL KNOWL-

EDGE, INCES', fathers wit' they own chi'ren, RAPE!
Beastly-ality. YES! BEASTLY-ALITY! And de MEN?
Where are de men? NO FATHERS! Allelujah, oh yes.
Look around you-ah ...

A woman come in front on the screen saying how all
them people behind she in a party having a good time,
while she out here with gas. No shame. She take a tablet.
'Not any more!' she say.

'Aye! Da preacher need one'a dem tablet, boy. Tek-out
all he gas, ha!'

Lynette don't ketch Ossi joke. Is only when Ossi open
he mouth that Lynette watching at what going on. De
preacher man pulling she mind. Reminding she about
things she don't want to think 'bout. Even me can see that
on she face. She thinking 'bout Baby Keisha.

The girls down in the water admiring sea things: sea
fans, sea feathers, sea frost. I know all'a them same things.
Li'l fish passing and then the music changing, heavy, a
man with a knife down there too. But they don't see
him. The darky music getting louder, they swim into a
undawater cave still admiring the place: 'Gee, this is fan-
tastic! It's so peace-full.' The t'iefing fella digging round
the treasure box with he knife. 'Wow ... let's take a
picture before we go.' They have the camera down in the
water and all. The man setting a undawater dynamite ...

Watch who leading you! De blind leading de blind,
sweet Father in heaven-ah ... De politicians there telling
you de same STUPIDNESS! A EXCUSE! A excuse canna'
save you, it canna' save yuh chi'ren! Only Gaad can do
dat, Amen. When t'ings bad, they tell you is Trinidad
fault, Trinidad ain' giving we enough money. Or is de
Amerrycans controlling we. Before dat, was de British.
They telling you watch dem foreigners coming in, de

Germans buying land, big hotel going up. Always some-
body else fault, never they own . . . and YOU SIT DOWN
LIKE A MOO-MOO LISTENING! AMEN! You ain'
see where de money going? You ain' seeing NUTHING!
Nuthing-ah! Satan'self could be in yuh house and you ain'
go see HIM-AH . . .

The girls smiling for the camera in the cave. The
wick t'ing burning to the dynamite. Undawater. The man
swimming fast away . . . Booush!

'Dem girls go get trap, boy . . .'

Rocks falling down on them, they hold on together,
mouth round. The hole for them to get out block up. No
air. They air running out. Ceejay feeling faint, start closing
she eye.

Look where yuh chi'ren going . . . give dem a better
life, hallelujah. Before is too late, too late, too late-ah!

The coastguard fellas done notice the girls' boat on
top, notice they missing too long.

'Dey coming, girl. You ain' go dead!' Ossi admiring
the fellas, how they ever-ready. Coastguard fellas pulling
out the rocks with a boat cable, giving the girls air.
Carrying them up to the surface. On top the water the
others done ketch the t'ief. 'Oh, wow! How can we ever
thank you guys enough?' The two fellas holding them,
smiling big, Ossi too. The girls bouncy selves, floating
round the fellas' necks in the water. 'I'm sure we can think
of a way!'

Lionheart with Van Damme showing later. Fire blazing
behind the man naked steely chest, face scrench-up,
kicking. Aagh. Gun down five fellas . . . aagh. Lynette get
up and go outside.

Dem People

The old pumps and the roof on the jetty quiet this afternoon. Ossi, Dexta and Kerwin liming on the jetty, me in
the water on the mash-up surfboard, floating. Dem people
park they car where they always does and walk slow up
the jetty holding hands and a basket. They stop halfway
to the end, watching Ossi and them jump-diving, spread
something and set down. The lady take off she slippers
and swing down she foot over the edge. The mister' big
chest lean forward over the water. I rest my chin on the
board and set out for Stompy boat. Looking back, I see
both they heads turn to me skimming out.

The glitterwater all round me. Twinkling and shimmying, tippling me in Stompy boat. I set there a long while
feeling the last'a the sun making salt on me skin. A big-
size pelican plunge quick straight out from the sky, right
next to the boat, cork back up to the surface with 'e beak
lock-down. Bubbing gentle, the little sticky-out feathers
behind 'e head ruffling. Li'l round eye staring me down
to see if I know if he have a fish in he beak or not. A
t'iefing gull attack, land on 'e back and make the pelican
gulup the fish, jerking 'e pocket up and down. The
pelican lift up off the water, flapping and beating off the
gull, dripping and shining over me head, beak glinting and
zipping back in 'e Z-shape.

More pelicans diving by the Bocas Rock, the t'iefing
gulls screaming and wheeling between them. Waves out

there breaking orange on the rocks, rolling in slow-motion, white foam turning pink from the sky. The shadow-water by the land deepen blacker and I now can see the sun setting behind me without looking round. The big tamarind tree turning from green to gold. The lady white dress on the jetty go pink, and a small cloud high up, pink too. Everything shining out before going to sleep. Even the rusty old roof and pumps trying to shine. And the sky behind Plymuth going far away, up higher still and deeper smooth blue. Another sweet-skin night come.

Ossi wave to me. He dark against the sky. He going. I slide onto the surfboard, untie it and stretch out. Darkness coming quick now. Stroking my arms through the warm silky water, it waggle my fingers when I trail them. Feel it licking my skin. Dem people still sitting on the jetty. I tie up by the rusty ladder and dip a last time in the kissy water before I pull myself up. The two'a them watching out where the sun gone down. I pick up me shirt and start up the boards. They look up at me as I pass.

'Goodnight.'

''Night.'

Looking down on the lady face I feel extra tall and slim 'cause I know she eye stretch from me foot right up to me face. And smiling. The mister smiling too. I don't know if they can see me smiling. Or me eyes slinking down the lady neck. The goodnight sky pulling me head up, stretching me back long and smooth, stroking the sea water down off me legs and heels, slicking on the planks every step. Carryin' me right home.

*　　*　　*

The lady was real easy to talk to, boy. Even though was Ossi did the talking. We see she down in Sunday School fête, one Sunday night. I was real surprise to see she down there. She dancing-up inside Paris Rumshop and then 'cross the street in the fishing shed where the fête more hot-up. Dancing with the fella who father own the big hotel, with he and he friends. He does always have plenty friends round he. She was dancing with other fellas too. And laughing and moving all the time to Buju, Beenieman and all them songs. When Bob Marley come on, she skanking like a fella. Straight jeans and t-shirt, she almost look like a fella too – if wasn't for the hair.

When she come outside the shed, standing close up to we, Ossi tap she shoulder. Boy, when she turn round, she face shining up at me, making me feel tall again.

'You from Plymouth!' She reco'nised we. 'Hello, I'm Bella.' Shake Ossi hand and then she was shaking mine, hard. 'You're twins?'

I look at Ossi and smile, still feeling tall and swayey.

'What's your name?' She shout over the boom-bass. Coming closer. 'I've seen the two of you in Plymouth on the jetty.'

She stand 'longside us, leaning across me to hear Ossi, not minding she shirt touching me drinks arm. He laugh, roll back he head to the music and lift up he Guinness bottle. She smile and start rocking in time. Ossi could do that, he could know what to do and what to say, just so, any time. I stand cool. Waiting for me words to come. *Always be de best, there's no life in de West.* Ossi rolling he head. *Propaganda dem'a press, times will have to confess.* I wanted to watch she face close-up. *Monday mornin' living is a mess.* Then she dash back under the shed, bouncing with them fellas. One hold-on on she and the two'a them raise they hand hailing, *an' all'a dem stylie, stylie, sty-lay. In'a de party, party, part-ay.* Wining they waist together go down. *An' all'a dem sexy, sexy, sex-ay.* A next fella hold-on behind, she rub-a-dub the both'a them. *De gyal dem'a bother me, botha' me, botha' mey.*

I watched she getting on with them fellas. Wild-up, jamming up close close with them. And two'a the fellas ugly boy, Tarzan and Rambo. You ain' want to see they face in the day nuh. Two renk gigolo fellas from Canaan, always ketching tourist girl. The rich-man son introducing she to more a'them. She can barely see they face proper but shaking they hand like a man, buying drinks. She disappear gone in the thick black centre'a the shed. Oiling-down with the big lump'a bodies. In there does be clampy, man tie round woman, bumsey and breast pasting you down. Girls don't mind what on they bumper. Pusspiration running high, hot and sweaty. *Hold a gyal and give she, gi' she jukie-jukie. Hold a man and give he, gi' he jukie-jukie.* The bass in there does pump up you blood, thunder you chest. Battie-rider short pants riding, pum-pum shorts rolling, pedal-pushers pushing.

She reach back out on the edge'a the dark lump'a dancers, chuffling and singing, a fella leading she by the hand, she jab he shoulder and start wining with he right there. In front'a we. Ossi, busy with a girl, roll' he eyes by me. The fella Bella dancing with is a battie-man. Like she don't care. They turned back to back and grind bumsey, she bend-over laughing.

'Boy, go and akse she for a dance, boy!' Ossi shout.

But I was still waiting to gather some belly. *Under the Sycamo' tree, under the Sycamo' tree, de young gyal'a bow unda' me.* I just start to thaw-out, swinging, swaying, grooving. She was watching me. *De young gyal'a bow unda' me . . .*

Then she leave and go 'cross to Paris, the back-in-times dancehall.

Ossi eye ketch me. 'Un-unh! I ain' going 'cross there.'

So I find meself there alone and when I reach, wasn' no sign'a Bella. White hats, bright teeth and eyes cruising to Barry White. I strain me eye all about the corners in the purple light room, black walls on one side, a woman white shoes stepping. The other side open up, big-size couples crooning, the big voice drawling. I check for she in Jimi Hendrix bar, still wasn' no sign. Brace-up on the speakers and then I see she. Coming from the toilet outside. One'a the ugly fellas, Tarzan, had excort she out there, he coming down the steps with she and same time James Brown start *Get up, get on up. Get up, get on up.* If you see them moving. *Yaow. The way I like it, is the way it is.* Head wagging, bendy bouncing they weave they way 'cross the dance floor. *An' like a sexxmachine. Unnh.* She spot me in the corner. Tarzan thighs copying hers, touching hers. He shorter than she. She raised a hand and pull back she curls, eyes touched mine clear through the dark. *An' like a loverrmachine.* The big-size couples squeeze up closer together, head rest on a shoulder, heavy arms 'cross the top of a bumsey. *Sex-youall healing.* I sweeten me mouth for she but she could'na see that. *'Cause you do it right. Baye-bee.* Dancing with the fella but she ain' hold-on tight. Rocking and smoothing we eyes into one, them slow words melting all round. Maybe the next dance . . . then, bram – *One o'clock, two o'clock, three o'clock rock.* People lash out twisting, skirts flying, plenty white teeth flashing and she and the fella slap each other, run laughing out'a there. She jump on he back, meet

39

up with he partners, they jockey Tarzan too, gone horsing up the road.

Them gone, all that left to watch was them big people with they old-time dancing in Paris. Back over by Ossi, them Rastas with they head tight on weed, there liming with the shadows by the beach. A few more quick-talking gigolo fellas hooking up some white girls, working hard, shamming and showing-off to them, hoping the girls go take them for the night, or a week. A couple'a Tomo fellas by the bar but they wouldn't even show as if they know me, not when they chilling. Ossi start pulling the girl into the dark mess. 'Wait fuh me, eh!' he bawl out to me.

* * *

Soon as Mudda reach home, Lynette start.

'You ain' seeing what really going on with dese chi'ren! What dey doing when dey roaming whole day?'

'Who? Wha' happen?'

'Ossi! Wha' happen? He servicing de whole'a Plymuth!'

Mudda stop in the kitchen doorway and look at Lynette knocking about in the kitchen with Keisha on she hip side. The hot Scarbro lines lift off from Mudda face for a minute.

'Ossi?'

Ossi out the back bathing.

'Yeah, dat same Ossi! Charlotte mudda and she neighbour had a fight today. Two big women like dat, cussing out they business for de whole worl' to hear, who fucking who man. De neighbour pelt a bucket on Charlotte mudda and den they start. Everybody in Plymuth stan' up and watch dem. Two big woman. Rolling and kicking, tearing up one 'nother clothes. All they panty tear, big battie flopsing out-a-door. Charlotte mudda hold de neighbour hair and wreng it round, rip off de woman extension! Dey cuss and bawl fuh a hour and who name in de midst'a all dat? Ossi! I never shame so. Ossi was right there too, wid he mouth heng-open watching.'

'Ossi? Charlotte mudda?'

'Yes! De neighbour cuss Charlotte mudda 'bout how she daughter is a whore. An' then how she know how Charlotte mudda fuck she own daughter boyfriend too. Ossi!'

'Whea boy.' Mudda eyes lighten. She look ready to smile. 'Ossi?'

'Ossi! And when de neighbour finish cussing 'bout how Charlotte *and* she mudda fucking Ossi, making he more magger like a dog, she turn round and say how them is dogs too 'cause Ossi is she left-left – she fuck Ossi already!'

'Oooy! Oh Lawd. Ossi!' Mudda can't hold it in no more, she buss out laughing, hitting the post with she palm and shaking she head. 'Ossi!' She call out to him splashing under the pipe. He listening all the time, hearing every word. 'You boy!? Hooy!'

Ossi laughing to heself, hanging he head down under the pipe and sucking in water running down he face.

'Hooy! Look at my crosses!'

'You laughin'! Laugh good.' Lynette warned. 'When he swell somebody girl-child belly, see how you go be laughing then.'

But Mudda done reach by the outside door, watching Ossi bathing.

'Ossi, you good yes! Look at you. All de time I t'inking you riding yuh bike wit' Cliff and is *dat* you riding? Boy!' She hoot again and turn inside.

He hanging he head more and smiling a goat smile.

White with soap, sudsing it up all over heself and round he crotch. Pipe water splattering big frothy lumps on the rusty-colour concrete and the eat-away bottom of the galvanise. I watch him take off he shorts, rinse them and wring-out them over the concrete drain. He standing dripping in front of me.

'Pass da towel fuh me.' He face still have the goat smile when he look up at me.

I just watch him and steups. Leave him standing there stamping the water off he foot, biting he bottom lip. He don't know what to do with heself or he long totee. Just doing what the girls and them want he to do, and he feel that is it. Me, I make for different. Lynette going to rant and rave for the rest'a the night. And Mudda find it a joke, she li'l boy turn man. Brush past Mudda sitting in the kitchen still laughing to sheself, and leave the house. Walk down to the junction and set down. Ossi li'l friends there but they don't akse me nuthing. I don't say nuthing. They know Ossi ain' coming out tonight. Everybody just goat-smiling the whole night when they watch me. Hardly any cars pass. Tomo and he fellas in Scarbro tonight. I ain' have no money to reach Scarbro.

*　*　*

Stompy drop me off on the rocks before he gone. Watch me through the water before he move off, a white-bubble silence left behind with me. A kind'a quiet you can only find in the sea. Even in them li'l pools up on the rocks, or just climbing around at the bottom of the cliffs catching crabs – the sea does give you the same kind'a peace. Floating over fancy colours and waving sea fans, kind'a plants you can't imagine God would put there, does make you forget what you come for. Something moving on the shiffing seabed but the white bubble still hanging, I don't go down to look. A lobster back-back under a rock, and some sergeant fish come sweeping round the corner. Bubbles carrying me soft. Past the big coral brain where I bounce-up a moray eel once. A rain'a blue and silver flecks ripple over me head. The bubble come up with me breaking for air, ears crackling with surface breeze, guluping and going down again.

The first silence gone. Now, the clear crunch-crunch of the clowning parrot fish biting the coral just below, scratching my ears. They always look so foolish, the parrot fish. Never blink. Make-up always fix, floating around looking at everything and eating all the time. Yellow-ring eye looking at you, mouth crunching, paint-on green lips, look like a fat lady smiling while she eating. Two more parrot fish gossiping. I juk at the crunching one, it freeze for a minute then turn away. Touch the sharp skin of a star coral, clear slime leave a jelly feeling on my fingertips. Current pulling me gentle away and forward – to the tall weeds waving. Low down, fleshy orange plops pulsing, open. Touch them too. One by one and watch them close. Closing up like goat battie-hole. Feel like it too. I blink me own battie-hole, it make you want to do that, watching them. They stay tight and squinge-up till I move away.

Surface, take air and go back down. Again and again. Looking for different things each time. Touching, jabbing. Upside down, pushing my head under a coral shelf, me body swaying upwards like the weeds. A spider crab spread 'e legs and peep out from the dark under there. I push the tip of me spear gun in and scrape it on rock, the scratch loud and raw in the water. Not much of a silent-hunting feeling today. Not much stirring 'part from the powdery sand at the bottom, frilly weeds and the floating parrot fish. One start champing again.

As I pull meself out on the rocks – voices. A tremble jump from me belly to me mouth. Is dem people there, so close. They spot me head push up. Me eye butt-up with the lady own and I straighten up.

'Hi there,' she say first.

I don't look at she too much. The mista turn round. They stay turn round and watching me so I have to go up to them, even if I don't know what to say. Crouch down next to them on the sand-rocks, almost the same colour as the mista hair. Sun putting some blood back in me sea-soak skin.

'G'afternoon.'

'Peter, this is . . . what's your name again?'

'Cliff.'

The mista stick he hand out. I put my hand in it and he shake it twice. Palm smooth and white, tight skin. Square strong fingers, clean, with goldie hair on the top sides. He hook them back round he knees.

'You been out there long?'

'Long? Un-huh. Yeah.'

'We been here a while too. You catch anything?'

'Na.' I don' look at her.

The mista watching the sea. It reflectioning on he glasses and he eyes colour with the sea too. I stroke a white line in the sand-rock and watch the grains roll down. Sea heffing and puffing gentle down below. A loud drooly noise come from a hole close to the mista foot. We all look to it and laugh.

'It sounds like it wants to suck his toes!'

I laugh out then. Imagine he big white toe in the hole

and the sea sucking like a baby cow, slurk, slurk, slurk. The mista laugh too and wave he big toes.

They was here all the time I was diving. Set down in the same spot I does come to breathe with the sea. I sure if they look in me eye now they could see what I was seeing. But they both looking at the sea again. A pelican swoop in faster than the wave washing under it and they heads follow it. The way they sitting there so quiet, I can't guess what they dreaming 'bout, what colours they can find in the sea. When they look at the hills, what they know? The house-backs'a Plymuth, how it look to them? Sun shimmy on the water and blink-up on the mista glasses and de lady face.

'It's a nice view 'eh?' she say, quiet.

I look around. A 'view' they call it. I can't say if it nice, I been seeing it every day since I born. So I say nuthing.

'You come here a lot?'

I nod.

She squinny her eye and look at me.

'I live over dere.' I point to the back'a the houses. 'Allyou live in Tobago?'

'Yes. We live just past Arnos Vale, on the hill over the bay.'

I watch she feet.

The mista press he hand down and shift he body. 'These rocks are hard on your arse!'

Hear the way he say 'arse'!

'Where's your brother?'

'Ossi? He home or somewhere.'

'Youall could pass and visit us some day, yes?' She look at the mista.

'Yes, come around some time if you'd like.'

'Yeah. Un-huh. A'right.' Me they talking to, eh! Hear things. 'Come around some time if you'd like'. Visit them. Is me they talking to. Not no small boy, no poor-ears fella from Plymuth. Like as if I have me car and house same like them. They couldn'a be from here nuh.

I smile and watch them looking out still. We stay there watching the sea 'view', them seeing it how they want and I seeing it how I always does.

* * *

The next time I see dem people, me and Ossi was riding round in Carnbee. We had on we good clothes and the sun was cooling off. They stopped the car and we went right up to them. Ossi so bold-face, while I looking over me peepers, he akse the mista outright, 'When to pass?'

'Well, tomorrow if you like.'

'Tomorrow, Saturday. 'Bout three o'clock?'

'Yes, that's all right.'

'Awright. We go make a pass. Right Cliff?'

I was looking past de lady bare leg. Was a black phone in the car. 'Un-huh. Yeah.'

Both a'them had on they shades. The mista hair blowing around and touching the roof in the car, glass on top open. Me and Ossi circle and dodge in front a'them before wheeling off down the road. My shirt rippling 'gainst my belly and the sea feeling rise up in me. Ossi teeth shining, we flashing and we feel dem people watching we, they and they car with a phone, smooth skin and soft hair, smiling and waving. Down to me foot feel good. From then till Saturday.

* * *

Up, down, top ranking.
Love is all I bring
In'a me khaki suit and t'ing.
I pop nuff style.

And cool all the while. Them old-time reggae song know 'bout slow style, and is that playing in me head now as we turning in we gap. It does help you chip and curl when you walking. A shoulder-rolling slow style.

Ossi hustling in front, rushing to go run he mouth. Watch he. He awright, yuh-know, I like he with me dear heart but he mouth like to run too much. Lynette is the first one he go tell. When he finish, it going out on the block, through he li'l friends to the whole'a Plymuth. Hear he nuh. 'Dem people invite we, boy! Lynette, yuh know dem people who does pass in da fancy car, a white man and a lady? Dem. We going by dem tomorrow.'

Lynette ain' watching he, she checking me face.

'Is up so they living. They invite we to pass by they house. Must'e a big-shot house. Dem rich, yuh-know. Big-time people. It have a phone in they car.'

'Whe' they from, Cliff?' She aksing me.

'Me ain' know nuh.'

'De lady must'e Trini and the mista is a English. En't Cliff? He sound like a English.'

'And just so they invite you?'

I ain' telling Lynette nuthing. She ain' checking Ossi, is me alone she watching.

He still excity. 'And wha' wrang with dat? Da' is how dem kind'a people does move, yuh-know. Hear: de mista: "That's fine. We'll be expecting you then." Aye! No joke, 'eh.'

'Ossi, you going wit' Cliff, right?'

'Of course! Is me who talk to dem. Three a'clack, eh.'
All how they try, them ain' go cramp my style.

And no matter what yuh do
Yuh can't get thru
Unless you play de, play de, play de music.

Flim-style House

In front the house is a white wall. Peep through the slatty
wood door. Can only see the roof and garden and a gravel
path. Ossi press the bell and a broad fella come scrunching
out to the gate.

'Good afternoon. Come in.'

The place quiet. Me and Ossi push the bikes in and
soon as we step on the gravel we can see the long white
wall-house. Brace the bikes by two push-out jalousie
windows, the fella show us in and he go off down some
outside steps. The mista right there, coming towards us,
walking barefoot smooth on a white tile floor.

'There you are. Come in.'

For once Ossi don't know what to say. We look. You
can see all through the house. The kitchen right there
in the middle and you looking straight through to the
sea. Up and down the whole length'a the house is a white
inside walkway. We follow the mista into a room under a
tent. Bright white. On top the white tent is glass and the
front'a the room have no walls, just open balcony. Sun
blinding you off the white walls and white floor. And
railings. Big round white railings like a ship, all over in
the house. Not like no other house we never see. You
would'a never guess it so from the outside. Me and Ossi
don't say nuthing.

The mista set down on a white settee. 'Have a seat.
You rode here?'

Between the two settees is a carpet on some blue tiles. It look old and the edges nammy, but is still a carpet. Ossi look at we shoes, stretch heself on the edge'a the settee, leave he foot resting on the tiles. I look round and set on a dinner chair so I don't have to step on the carpet. The lady slink in barefoot silent from the walkway. She have on a bright orange short dress and she looking blacker in the all-white room.

'Hi there. You came! Cliff and . . . Ossi?'

'Un-huh, yeah.'

'Let me get you something to drink. You old enough to drink? Ha! Carib, juice, Coke.'

Even though we hardly never drink beer, Ossi lean back on the settee and say, 'I go tek a Carib.'

'Da' is wha'?' Ossi point up at the tent.

'The canvas? That's an awning. Before the glass roof was on, that was the roof! It can roll back.'

He get up and go out on the balcony. Me and Ossi follow. Glass going up shining with white steel things and wire inside the glass.

'Yeah, yeah, I see it. Is a glass roof in true, boy. And da' is wha'?' Ossi point to the piece'a wall along the front of the house. It look like coral with black moss and ferns growing on it.

'It's cut coral. The blocks come from an old building.'

Ossi stretch he eye down the front of the house. 'Oh-ho. I see de design! Yeah. Is to make it look like a old-old house. Wha' they call it . . . ruins. Yeah. I see de design. Dat is a good one, eh? Anybody looking from so, go t'ink is a ruins! Dis house have plenty design.'

Hot sun on the white-ship balcony over the steep green hill. Feel like it just ready to set off and sail over the saman trees and down to the sea glittering out there.

De lady, Bella, come with drinks. Peeta put up he feet on the settee and lean back. Ossi watching he, rest he own bottle careful on the tiles between the settee and carpet and lean back on one elbow. They laughing with Ossi and we all trying to make comfortable. Bella set sheself on the edge'a the mista settee arm, legs stretching all the way along to the carpet. Ossi taste he beer slow, lean back and admire he Filas against the tiles. Inside that house make you feel like you on TV. All the colours showing up. My shirt feel whiter, me pants feel bluer. I look at me Nikes setting there on the clean floor. Look like it wasn't my foot, is a shiny photo, a ad. Michael Jordan or one a'them fellas.

The small boy come from the kitchen side and stop behind Ossi settee.

'Oliver, come and meet Cliff and Ossi.' The mista stretch out he arm and the boy come and brace-up on he settee.

'Hi. They twins or what?' He look from Ossi to me.

Both'a we smiling.

'Un-unh. Na.' Ossi smile and rake back some more in he settee, turning up he face.

'You not twins?' Bella look long at his face, then mine.

'Na.'

'Who's the oldest? You.' She ketch me eyes over the peepers before I look down.

'He twenty, yuh-know.' Ossi mouth.

'Twenty!' The mista laugh. 'You look much younger.'

The small boy look at Ossi from he Filas to he basket-ball shorts, to he Chicago Bulls jersey, bandanna round he neck and corn-row hairstyle. Then he turn and watch me same way. Watching me straight in me face, taking in the visor and peepers. I watch him through me blue glass.

'Wha' happenin' dere, small boy? Gimme a bounce.' Ossi stretch out he fist and the boy come forward, touch he knuckles to Ossi own and go back to he father settee.

'So soft man? Gimme a real bounce, nuh.'

He come and cuff Ossi fist.

'Right. Right.' Ossi take another taste and set up.

'So what youall fellas do?' Bella akse.

'Nuthing much.'

'No work?'

'Yeah. Cliff does work. Down de road in Black Rock wit' de cycle shop.'

'And you?'

'Nah. I ain' get nuthing yet. Cliff does go out fishing with a fella, Stompy. Not me, nah. Roasting in da hot sun all day, making you skin black and cripsy, hand hard like leather, all you mouth crack up. Every chances he get, he like to go by the sea. There in it like a fish. Da' na' for me nuh!'

'So you don't like snorkelling and so on?'

'Sea is fuh fish. Not for me. I like jumping jetty wit' dem boys, but dat is it.'

I watch him and laugh. 'He don' like nuthing to do wit' de wata. He don' even like bathin'!'

Bella akse if we want to see the rest'a the house. Start from one end with a bathroom in the open air – no roof. We follow she floating down the walkway, peeping in rooms. At Peeta and Bella bedroom, a thing jump we. Both me and Ossi.

'Wha' da'?'

A black boy stand up in there silent, arm stretch up resting on he head, looking out to the sea.

'Make me jump!' Ossi looking closer.

Now I see that the boy is a dolly. But he naked. Full-size and real-life. That is what jumbie we.

'Da''s a dallie?'

'A dolly? It's a sculpture. A sculptor friend of ours made him. Beautiful, eh?'

'Wha' it make out'a? Wood?' Ossi in the room going round it.

Not me, I watch it from the door and it stay watching out.

''E skin don' look like wood. Watch nuh Cliff. Wha' 'e have dere?' Pointing to where the crotch bump out. 'Could be a girl, en't? But how somebody could make a t'ing so?'

'Hilda, the woman that carved it . . .'

'A woman make dat?'

'She had a name for it but her workmen called it *Little Black Boy*, from Gypsy's calypso last year. You know the song?'

'Un-hunh.'

Bumsey small and high, legs tight and shining, down to 'e foot real as life, standing same size as a shadow, silent as a jumbie. *Little Black Boy*. Could'a be me or Ossi when we was young, or any li'l flat-chest girl bathing by a standpipe.

After that she show we the next surprise, a bathtub and shower on a balcony sticking out clear over the trees. And as we passing back down the walkway, even though I know the black dallie in the room there, 'e still make me stop, look again. As if it go move and hide. As a spirit does make you look back.

In the settee room, Ossi aksing questions and talking. De people look at me sometimes for me to talk, but Ossi watch me and open he mouth most times. Ossi talking he talk. And I know he go talk he talk in Plymuth too.

'Peter likes sailing,' Bella say.

'Oh-ho. A Sunfish?'

'Something like that. You know anything about sailing, Cliff?'

'Yeah man. I like it. I sail them Sunfish a'ready.'

'I don't like it,' Bella say. 'Those little things tip over in no time. And you have to be fighting-up with ropes, banging up yourself all over.'

Ossi guffaw loud, rolling around. 'Fuh true! Is true. Not me!'

'It's good fun,' Peeta say.

I watch him direct. 'Is good fun, en't Peeta?'

The small boy disappear and I can see Bella looking at me between talking. I watch she too. And the mista. They look bright-up like they on TV, 'cept neither one a'them perfect-looking all over. Talking and sipping. The mista put he hands behind he head and touch de lady leg with he toes. I like to hear how he talking – like the fella who does them animal programmes but he don't whisper all the time.

We starring now. I move me famous foot. You know how much people go pay for me two-foot to be in a ad? For me to wear a Nike trackpants? Thousands'a US dollars. Better yet if I smile and say 'Just do it'. Millions. I watch me brother, Magic, relaxing, chatting in the talk-show. Everybody like he. But I have the looks. Watch me nuh.

After all the talk we talk, a chatting conversation, dem people make we relax in the TV set. Them ain' stiffy or poshy like them uppa-class people. They like to make joke and laugh. Youth-man joke too, not no old mannersy behaviour. Just how they friendsy-looking, that's how they is. I never meet people so, boy. They son and all like we. They even akse if we want to go for a drive tomorrow. A drive, yuh-know. Hear the li'l boy, Oliva: 'That's so boring, not a drive!'

* * *

Flashing going in the car. Immortelle trees – red clouds passing over glass roof. Big bamboo stands, black 'n' white stripe road-walls drumming . . . sjuup . . . sjuup . . . in between. Passing Moriah, quite up on the ridge. The fat trunk'a the jumbie tree sjupping past close-up to the road. We flashing with the sun . . . Sun is shining . . . The weather is easy . . . Skimming 'long the grey road, curving and cutting round the hilltops . . . Makes you want to move . . . Yuh dancing feet . . . A silver bullet. Silent.

A cud-chewing cow watch us fly past and blink. Must be how you does feel inside a plane. Smooth steel. Sea far away down, silver too and shimmering. Dark cloud patches making map on it. Banana and cocoa crouching down in the valley and them lonesome gru-gru beff trees stop in they march up the grass hills. Sjuup, sjuup. Two house holding onto the roadside and looking back – down the drop to the ravine and the sea. Past Castara. Coasting.

A Bigger Room

Past Castara. Cliff and Ossi relaxing in the back seat. Past Norman Parkinson's house. Round the bend where the sea suddenly blinds you. Right there. A whole sweep of glittering blue stretching to God and beyond. And us, streaking, skirting, clinging to the slope. Downhill. Parting the flesh of the valley. A hidden grazing field. Gentle almond trees shading the river . . .

Cliff and Ossi arrived yesterday. I heard the bell ring. Heard Thomas, our caretaker, go out to let them in. Through the Demerara window slats I saw them bracing bikes, heads looking around. Peter took them through to the living room.

. . . Level with the blazing scaly sea. Rock face leaning over us speeding, dripping green-vine envy. The freedom of an ocean in me. Sailing.

I went to join them, eyes seeing before I reached, mouth talking before I was ready. Three long bodies unfolded. Cliff's curved into a director's chair. Peter's arms spread along the length of his settee and Ossi twisted like a rope onto the tiles. Faces tight trying to control and be cool, bodies automatically posing. In this light, the bright-up room was a vivid painting. Black skin silhouetted against white walls, blue-striped cushions and yellow canvas chairs. The pants, the sneakers, the visor and shirt said 'Nike', out of place in this David Hockney bigger room.

New eyes stretching up to the roof, the canvas and the glass, taking in the strange doors and pieces of walls. I'd seen the surprise on people's faces before. The openness of the house made people look at you different after they'd seen it. In one glance down the long white corridor they saw the swing of my walk, how my arms hung, the white of my teeth. It let them see right through my clothes and see my whole self, where the sweat forms under my breasts, the dent on my chest bone. Showed me their insides too, and I could see their different selves in the way they stared. Some selves peeped out, others ran deeper inside. Cliff didn't want to look past the shower to see how we would be bathing out in the open, embarrassed, just tucked his head down. Ossi exclaiming and spinning around.

Ossi doing the talking. Lips and eyelashes curled back like a girl's as he talked. A dimple twinked when he smiled suddenly and his long beautiful face swung round on his neck like a mask, looking up, out, turning to Peter, straight at me. Cliff's pure beauty bounced my eyes away. His shyness slipped up and over the blue shades trying to hide his smile spreading, lip-chewing, hand fidgeting. Uneasy with his own grace. Ossi checking Cliff's uncertainty but it only made him pose more, talk more, admiring his sneakers the whole time. Weren't twins at all, but they had a way of looking to each other all the time. Ossi laughing, 'Teheh!' and asking all the questions: how long we living here, we married, what work Peter does? Peter struggled to explain.

The handsome tone of the afternoon relaxed them. And us. Heat leaked slow out of the sun and they stretched, walked right up to the rail on the terrace and took in the view before going. Long limbs rolled them out the door ready to bring them back for a drive, next day.

'They're really nice, those young chaps.' Peter was grinning. 'Sense of humour too.'

'And so good-looking!'

'I know. Both of them. Cliff's features . . . he looks like *Little Black Boy*.'

'He does too. Nubian Nike.'

'But they do seem nice. I like their slanty style! Couldn't see a trace of "attitude", even though they're from Plymouth. When you think of the kind of fellas you usually see hanging around there . . .'

Oliver came round the corner. 'The cool dudes gone? You saw his earring said Nike? And his hairstyle, man! Picky-picky on top and something shaved on the back. You didn't see that? They real cool, eh?'

I had watched Oliver inspecting them, their style and movements. His little chocolate face, intense but friendly. Sapodilla-seed eyes shiny, inquisitive. Mopsy curly hair and clothes anyhow, his bold questions and chat amused Cliff and Ossi. Made him perform more, playing up to the 'real' cool dudes right here in his home.

Just Peter and I in the living room then, reading after dinner. Oliver in bed. The afternoon painting framed in our heads. Bold colours and figures so close, still warming my blood.

'I'll enjoy going for a drive up the coast tomorrow. We haven't done that in a long—'

'I know what you're thinking! You're wetting your pants!'

I sprang on Peter but he had got it out before I reached him. 'I'm not! How you could say that!'

'You are!' Laughing chin stuck up in the air. 'Go on. You're thinking, "Umn, nice and tall!" ' Scrunched up his fingers like I would be grabbing somebody's balls, jumped his eyebrows up and down. 'Very nice!'

'No, you stupidy!' But I was laughing too.

We laughed into the night. Peter kept teasing, sticking out his arm and feeling balls. Our stupidness together always surprised me. For all our different backgrounds it's the same silliness. Worse! I still have hang-ups, trying to prove myself to be something or the other, decent at least, but he's long gone past that. Completely ridiculous with each other, laughing with more love. That surprising sharing grew us into lovers soon as we met, came out any time, anywhere.

Now, when we share the same skin, a soppiness springs up, a tenderness and a sweet-sweet happiness swells out through the house like the smell of bread baking. Through day, through night. Through singing out of tune, cooking together with loud soul music playing, breakfast every morning. It grew Oliver more loving and laughing, makes him soppy too. He'll rub Peter's cheek and tell him when he needs shaving, still want cuddles and give you that sicky-sweet smile in bed. It keeps us together more powerful than any of us could have known. Even though Peter said he knew it first time he saw me, knew the feeling in his belly, he couldn't have known about sharing a skin. But the comfort of it, something this good, can't last for ever. I suspect that and I know he does too. But for nine years it has been and still is the powerfullest thing I could live for.

Look at him now, Peter. Driving with a passion. All in one with the steering. Smoothing us inland before rushing the next hill. Abreast it, cresting. Eagle eye circling. Winding down to Parletuvier nesting there. Easing into the village. Cool drinks from Brother Michael's shop. Fishermen liming on a doorstep and the road ending at the closed-up school on the beach.

Parletuvier

Parletuvier always made you go quiet and dreamy, your soul melting out through eyes and skin. A place where silent hills turned indolently at the clouds' commands, changing from the untouched and compelling beauty of a child's flawless face to hunched brooding shadows of a tortured ancient. Today the bay dazzled clear blue and strong as we reached the end of the jetty. A pure sand beach wiped a semicircle clean. Wooden houses clustered on the sand, others strayed, speckling up to the first ridges of rich rainforest. Knitted tight as African hair, hills stretching back and up. Beyond them the dark centre of 'The Melancholy Isle'. A distant eye, grey-green and cataract, never forgetting, still looking out for sailors venturing its coast, scanning for ships with their black cargo approaching from the north. Tobago ... 'a mass of lofty, gloomy mountains with black precipices descending abruptly to the sea'. The eye, clouded with hate and the burning flesh of slaves, barely able to discern the scars left on its shores – Bloody Bay, Man of War Bay, Englishman's Bay, Granby Fort. The bones of old estates: Mason Hall, Franklyn's, Old Grange, Runnymede, Whim. Sullen embers of revenge still smouldering up there, smoking under the wet clouds.

Visiting from Trinidad, we could never have seen the darkness of this island. The strength of it overpowered and silenced you. Only after moving here did the calm become unsettling. Traces of resentment under the skin of proud faces, in the gait of mobile bodies. The house, our holiday haven from Trinidad city life, seduced us into its womb, promising peace of mind, crime-free living and the blue Caribbean sea. Once Peter's work in Trinidad had finished, we moved. And now the haven sheltered us from things unknown and deep. Always mothering, giving space for mistakes and meditation, watching over our sleep.

* * *

Ossi followed us out onto the jetty. Walked right up to the rowboat shell stranded on the end, climbed in and settled himself comfortably on the fishing nets. Took our towels and draped one over his head leaving just his nose sticking out.

'You going to sleep?'

'I ain' swimming.'

'You swimming, Peeta?' Cliff asked.

'I don't think so.'

'Well I am. I could jump in from here, can't I?' I looked down.

'Yeah man, 'e deep.'

It looked a long way down and I could feel the force of the water hitting me even before I jumped, crouched up and tensed. Soon as I plunged, uncurled and bubbled back up to the surface, I knew it was worth it. Peter waved at me and I went down again opening eyes under the water, eel-rippling. It's a clean kind of joy, to jump into cool water without touching sand. Makes you revel in it more. When the sun's splashing up with you, slicing rays through the water, it's a romping, clean joy. Under the jetty, dark ice water. I swam far out, drifting, floating, then pulled myself up the ladder near Peter. Ossi with my shades on, comfortable as ever in his towel-cowl look, legs crossed. I got some shots of him fooling about, Peter and Cliff chuckling.

Ossi grinned and took off the shades. 'Dem t'ings does hurt me eyes, nuh!'

'But it looking good!'

'Eh-heh?' He put them on again, lay back and closed his eyes.

'So Peeta, you is a businessman?' Cliff asked cautiously.

'It seems so.'

'What you does do again?'

'Well, I advise companies about how they should protect themselves against certain risks. A kind of lawyer.'

'A lawya? So you does go in court and t'ing.'

'No, not much. I just advise companies. I'm a sort of corporate lawyer.'

'Oh, a corprate lawya. You does work for a cor-prashun.'

'No, I work on my own, that's how I can live out here and just travel to where I'm needed.'

I looked at Peter through the long lens. The light reflecting off the sea was catching the single strands of hair falling forward over his glasses.

'You ever see *Perry Mason?*'

'What's that?'

'It's an old American TV series. You must know it!' I put in.

'Yeah boy. Dat does have all kind'a case in it. He is a lawya and he does always ketch dem fellas, yuh-know! He real good, boy.'

'Uh-humn.' Peter agreed faintly.

Gazing into the clear water I remembered watching

Perry Mason in gentle black and white. His solid trustworthy face and heroic music filling the screen every time something dangerous was about to happen.

'So, you is yuh own boss man!' Ossi burst out from the towels, scrambling up from the boat. 'Da' is de life, eh Peeta! Wha', de man is a intanational man, yuh-know.' He stretched, lifted up his shirt and started rubbing his belly right in front of my face. 'Leh me see da' camera.'

I held it out for him to see.

'No, leh me take yuh pi'ture.'

'It's not easy to use,' I tried.

'Awright, I go just look through it.'

I handed it over carefully. 'Put the strap over your head. It's very expensive. Don't press anything.'

'Pose fuh me. Smile nuh! Watch me Peeta, holler cheese.'

You couldn't help but laugh. Him with the towel still over his head, posing off with the camera, slinging back himself.

'I could make a good photo-take-outer.' He handed the camera back over to me. 'What you does do wit' them photos? You does make plenty money?'

'No, it's a hobby really. I used to work in film.'

'Action flim? How? But hear nuh, you does tek-out dem pi'ture and make it look like foreign?'

I laughed. I knew the pictures he was talking about. Dressed-up babies sitting in front of a backdrop with a lake and autumn trees. Or snow-capped mountains with a boy standing in front, slicked down, sweating.

'No. I don't take portraits in a studio. And I *don't* take pictures like those!'

'Oh no! She's much more arty than that, man,' Peter laughed.

'So what kind'a pi'ture you does tek-out?'

Cliff was listening, looking far out.

'Anything I see that I like. People doing things they normally do. And buildings, places, things.'

Past Cliff's profile, the waves further out were spraying up over a humpback rock on the steep side of the bay. Washing right over it and then smashing into the backlash of another wave. Too far away to hear, stronger in the silence. Cliff's thoughts were floating out there too. Too far away to catch.

Peter looked up. 'I'm starving.'

* * *

We filed into the tiny restaurant back by the roadside.

'Is who driving dat nice-nice car?' The woman looked at me, then Peter. 'You?' She boomed out. 'Dat car real nice, yes.' Broad, standing behind a counter that came up to her huge chest. 'Allyou been here before! Is not de firs' time I seeing dat car. Yes, well I is Sandra.'

'I'm Bella and this is Peter.'

Her eyes moved on to Cliff and Ossi. 'What allyou doing up dis side?'

'You know them?' I asked.

'Yeah.' She watched Ossi as far down as she could see over the counter. 'Since they small boys I know dem. They related to Miss Lucy family.'

I looked to Ossi.

'Yeah, Miss Lucy live in Anse Fourmi. Yuh know how long I ain' been there!' Ossi looked to Cliff but he didn't speak.

'Un-humn. How yuh mudda?'

'She awright.'

Sandra looked from them to us. Slammed her arm down on the counter. 'Welcome to Riverside Restaurant. De *best* local food in Tobago.' She started pushing her way out past the counter. 'Allyou eating lunch? Is de *best*, yuh-know.'

I was looking for the river but all I could see was road. Bright chequered plastic tablecloths covered the few tables, and brown and orange lino covered the floor. Everywhere was hot plastic. A television stood in the corner with some plastic flowers on top and plastic vines drooped from plastic hanging baskets, speckled with fly spit. Shiny Carib Beer girls looked lustily at us from the posters by the bar, and Miss Guinness all bursting out of her tiger swimsuit, ready to bite 'de *best* fish'. Sandra looked down into my overalls past my swimsuit as I sat down.

'What you have for lunch, Sandra?'

'Fresh fish, de *best*. Snapper. And chicken.'

The brothers didn't want fish. 'We tired eating dat.'

Shandies, a Carib for Peter, water for me.

'Awright. Good.' Sandra clapped her hands to complete the order and started shouting to the kitchen. As she walked to and from our table with flowered place mats and glasses, the whole place shook. The boards sagged under the lino but they were used to her. Like her clothes. She came stomping back with forks wrapped in halves of paper napkins.

'Allyou went and swim.' She boomed from the bar. 'Sun hot, eh? It really making hot dese days.' She wasn't really looking for an answer or a conversation. Just an excuse to look directly at us. Started fanning herself with an exercise book. Watching.

King Peter's Dream

A bumping, dry dirt road draining dust downhill, left us at the stagnant river mouth, King Peter's Bay. The small bay empty, rocks curving out cupping the greenish water.
'Dis is yuh own bay, eh Peeta? King Peeta.'
'Oh I say, royalty, man!'
'But it doesn't look so good for snorkelling here.'
'Na man, it only looking so. De diving does be good. I ketch all kind'a t'ing here a'ready.'
Ossi looking for a shady spot on the beach to lie down.
'Peeta ain' diving?'
'Naw. I don't like it. Anyway I can't see a thing without my glasses. I'll have a swim though.'
'Yuh right, Peeta boy.' Ossi longed out his mouth and took off his shirt, spinning around looking for something to lie on.
Peter was already in, soaking and bobbing, his head and neck sticking right out. I went out to him, lifted him lying there, fish-kissed him with my mask on and started swimming out after Cliff.
Gliding fast through the water, flippers in slow motion, he paused for me to catch up. White water, white sand shifting, rising from a hazy seabed. Dark limbs and fins in the blue-green milkiness. His face came back towards me, hand quickly touched my arm, pointing out, deeper. Clearer, complete now, moving chest first, extended legs swaying above, his body even more elegant in the water.

Arms with big hands, barely attached at the shoulders, trailing behind. I struggled to stay in this dream. A shivery rush of a witness, part of a rare encounter. The magic intimacy of underwater contact, a dolphin gracing you for a moment. Vague weeds reached out and the cold currents stirred. A big brown fish stopped ahead. Cliff checked to see I was looking and it disappeared into the thick water.

Bursting for air we broke far out, close to where the rocks ended. Way back on the beach Peter was standing, Ossi sprawled.

"E rough eh?' Cliff shouted. 'De wata mix up.'

Pedalling water, choppy waves slapping, we scrambled with mouthpieces and started in along the surface. Wind, waves pushing in bursts, bumped us together, pulled us apart, easy as driftwood. Clumsy limbs knocking, embarrassing. I kicked to get ahead but he didn't seem to mind. Maybe didn't notice. Swimming alongside, closer, he gently took my hand, held it and pointed it towards the reef emerging from the white shallows. Small waves curled sheets of bubbles down. Undersurface billowing shiny silk, a half-filled parachute. We stayed there folded up. Cliff stretching out the back of his hand, white fingertips spread. Huddling together watching coarse sand grains settle and roll against his skin, rising, falling, forward, backward. Hairs on my arm swaying, gently tugging the same rhythm. Inside a snowflake paperweight, waiting for white specks to settle in our sealed sea-green dome. We the weightless plastic figures in it, rocking, mesmerised by our swirling kingdom. My shoulder bumped his chest, back brushed his stomach, stung me living again. A charge straight through me. Instant instinct pulled us apart and hurried us to shore. Peter was right there as I hauled myself out.

'What'd you see? What did you see out there? Anything exciting?'

'Not a damn thing,' I said and looked at Cliff. 'The water's all stirred up. Only a brown fish, couldn't even see that clearly.'

'So it does be sometimes,' Cliff said softly scuffing the sand, the white specks trapped in his springy hair.

'Not that! Does he have a big one?' Peter stamping and doing his hands like an accordion, eyebrows jumping as wicked as his eyes.

'Peter!' This man!

'Oh Gad!' Ossi rolling, pissing himself. 'Aye, Peeta!'

Cliff holding his laugh, grinning, sparking a wink at Peter.

'No? Well, you should have been here! This boy's been rolling around here all the time with his huge cock falling out!'

Ossi jumped off the rug spluttering, holding up his old boxer shorts. 'Peeta!'

'You have!'

We were all hooting laughing.

'Me, there am I trying to be decent and he's just sprawling off. In the shade too, it's not even like he's trying to get a tan!' Peter had even swum with his shorts on this time instead of stripping off.

'Whoo, Peeta! Da, sun hot, man. Me skin feeling hot.'

'Well go and swim!'

Ossi still laughing stumbled towards the water and then stopped at the edge.

'Go on!'

He ran and bombed himself into it with a shout. Came out a minute later trying to keep a straight face and hiding the front of his thin wet shorts.

We went right out on the rocks after that sudden ease. All of us smiling, Ossi in front till his pants could dry. Stepping on rough coral, out to the big boulders, then volcanic crags. Whipping salt blast as we rounded the tip and a roar spread out all round. Seawater surging into a deep, deep chasm. A gnashing, ferocious sea. Savaging. You had to look down into it, wait through the yawning for the next rush, salty breath and spittle spewing up in your face. The noise and hunger of it frothing. We gazed, breezing. Ossi's pants dried. Peter was looking around, hair flying, eyes lit up with the excitement of being perched over the churning gap. He looked up at Cliff, and Cliff quickly flicked his eyes out to sea. Land shyness creeping back over him even with all this wind and water around. I caught his eyes resting on my mouth, he worried his lip. Not smiling but not meeting my eyes, racing the roar of the sea in me. Ossi glanced at him and looked away. Peter too felt something unsettling the comfort of our laughter on the beach.

Night and Day

'Yeah. Is me, Cliff.'

'Where you calling from?'

'De payphone in Plymuth. I just call t'see how allyou doing.'

Calling to touch. To see how we feel after spending time together. Was it good, do we want to see them again? Don't know how to ask. Just smiling into the phone.

'Yeah boy . . . I awright. Just dere.'

I asked him if they wanted to come have dinner with us. 'Where's Ossi?'

'He dere.' But later Cliff arrived by himself. He mumbled something, ducking his head and plucking up the courage to take off his shades.

Sitting at the kitchen table he watched Peter washing and cutting chicken. Drew in a chest full of air, hesitating to talk again, softly, 'Yeah boy, Peeta. It good to be free sometimes, en't?' Cocked his head to see if Peter agreed.

'Who's tying you down?'

'Ossi nuh.'

'How?'

'He does always follow-follow me everywhere. All when I bathing, he like a . . . what de t'ing name? . . . a sucker fish. He stick on me like a sucker fish, man.'

Gave him some potatoes to peel.

'Me?'

'Yes, peel them and then cut them up.'

'Yeah boy, he does want t'know all me business. He does question me – "Whey you been?" "Who you been wit'?" Da' like a wife, eh Peeta?'

'Ha!'

I watched his splayed hands grappling with the potato peeler. Showed him how to use it. Him fumbling, Oliver bossing in, instructing, asking, 'You married?'

He laughed and bounced Oliver's shoulder with his. 'Ossi is de one who does help at home. If he could'a see me here now! Me, I does have to get away sometimes. And he does look fuh me! If he call, don' tell he I here.' He checked Peter frying an onion for the chicken.

I salvaged the manhandled potatoes, put them on and went for my shower. Steamy rain-fine spray, bathing me in the open, night air all around touching my skin. Was a kiss from the sky. Dark green leaves of the fiddlewood trees fingered the night silently and above the yellow coral-stone, the stars looked on. Each time was different bathing there. Fighting driving wind and rain, warm water slanting away. Or freedom-shine, sharing every part of you with sun and water on a blazing day. Take off the shower head and it became a standpipe. Soaping in the sun by the roadside or out the back of your house. Cliff's house. What kind of home? A threadbare towel. This bathroom the size of his bedroom? Leaving his home, alone down the empty backstreet to the dim streetlight. A blue phone box. Shadows liming in a group. Ossi calling out 'Aye'.

Voices rumbled warm out the kitchen, Cliff's deep accent and Peter's familiar bass. A rise in Cliff's tone, a strain, repeating himself slower. A question.

Night sky washing me, a small owl flew by. An under-white blur against rich black.

What does he want? Me? The house? The car? Nothing to do. Wanting to escape.

An exclamation. Apologising. 'Sorry I . . .' A rumbled reply from Cliff, then laughter. Peter's chesty laugh still bounced in my heart and I still noticed when it did. Now they're setting the table in the living room. Peter'd be placing his old white linen napkins, Oliver laying the forks and knives, hustling after Peter, chattering away. They had their own little ritual. Oliver trying to anticipate what's needed next, what wine, where's the corkscrew, pretending not to know, hiding it. Peter pretending to be puzzled, Oliver flashing it out triumphantly at the end of the performance, beaming pleased with himself and patting Peter's arm. A father–son time and tradition that sat with us round the table.

I lingered, warm water soaking into the sky. Suddenly Cliff stepped out on to the terrace straight across. He'd forgotten you could see clearly to the shower. His head flashed at me and then the falter – to turn round and go back into the living room, or pretend not to notice? He continued up to the rail and leaned forward, looking straight out. The same soft night caressing me came to rest on his shoulders, its fingers stroked his nose and lips. I turned my back to his figure lit gently against the black.

At the table we warmed with the food, even Cliff's awkwardness with his knife and fork couldn't shake our comfort. The chicken was good. Like Oliver, Cliff hung on Peter's words, tried to catch the joke, tapping the table laughing. He watched Peter teasing Oliver, checking his eyes for a twinkle, looked at his hands guiding his fork, square fingers pressing the tip of it down hard. Chewed a piece of chicken, sweetened his mouth and smacked his lips, half smiled, sly-glanced at me and helped himself to more. Was a new comfort he had with Peter, an uncertainty with me. The glass roof above reflected us sitting there, the lamp pouring down on Oliver, dark pink bougainvillea on the table, blue plates, wineglasses and silver cutlery winking.

'Yes.' Cliff finished eating, pushed back his chair and looked up at the reflection. 'It come just like a mirror, en't?'

* * *

Get on the bus. Get on the fucking bus!
Blue film light shivered on our faces.
Don' touch me man, don' touch me.
Who the fuck you think you are. You think you got any choice?
The big black man pushed the fella in handcuffs forward. A gleaming silver Greyhound stood waiting for them. Clapped him on the back and sent him stumbling.
Fuck you, man!
Yeah, that's what your father done to your mother, that's why you here in this shit. Wait till your pa gets here.
Ain' no fucking body gon' tell me what the fuck I can do.
His handsome black American face filled the screen with anger.
Cliff looked at me and then at the mirror roof. Us lying there on settees, the carpet, bottoms of our feet and walls flickering blue from the television screen. Sound bouncing off the glass roof and tiles, every *fucking* word clear. He turned and looked along his arm brushing the skin of my leg, casual but deliberate. Swung his head round to Peter. 'Peeta sleeping, yes.'

Lifted my head to look at Peter, hand spread on his bare chest, head slightly twisted, spectacles straining. Cliff's foot reached over and tapped the bottom of Peter's foot.

'De flim na finish yet, Peeta.'

'Oh no!' Straightening his head but not opening his eyes. 'Are they still *furking* this and *furking* that?'

Cliff laughed out, blue teeth flashing. The bus cruising on a long straight road, like only an American bus can do.

''E almos' done.'

'Umn.' Peter rubbed his chest and smacked his lips.

I looked at him a while, big hairless chest with the strange hollow in the centre, skin stretched taut. Smooth flat belly with a few hairs leading from his belly button down to the waist of drawstring pants. He peeped open his eyes at the TV, shut them again and lifted a foot up onto the back of the settee. 'Oh, God it's hot!'

Beetles banging against the bus still driving, a moth fanned itself on the corridor ceiling and the plant hanging over my shoulder yawned. Was hot. I sat up and shuffled the cushions. Theme music bringing on the credits. Cliff's arm still barely touching my leg, other hand resting on his stomach, shirt pulled up. Didn't dare move, couldn't know my feelings, much less know if Cliff felt anything too. He stayed still for the moment. I tensed.

Peter's eyes opened. 'Oh, good, it's done.'

Titles rolling, rolling, Peter rolled out of his settee and kicked at Cliff's foot, he still staring at the screen, stumbled out to the terrace and stretched. The movement unpinned me and I followed Peter, came up close behind hugging round his chest, arms sticking to his skin.

The videotape clicked into rewind, purring. Frogs

chirping like crickets in the warm blackness beyond the terrace rail. The dim lone coconut tree standing completely still, a witness to the heat. Peter turned, kissing my head gently. Bamboo leaves poised over the house, waiting.

'The sky's really clear tonight. See how many stars!'

Craning to look, he pressed me onto the rail. 'If I had better eyes I'd see them.'

'You must be able to!'

Straining, shading our eyes from the kitchen light.

Cliff came silently out onto the terrace, laid himself on the table looking up, shirt almost off, and Peter went for the stargazing mattress. I stayed hanging onto the rail, not looking at Cliff, not looking at anything, boring into the heavens. All the lights off, Peter and I lay staring up at the winky sky. Mattress breathing cloying soft all over us. Cliff sat up, pulled off his shirt and rolled his long back down onto the cool table top.

'Take off your shirt if you're hot,' Peter suggested.

'Me?'

Peter couldn't see my confusion? He couldn't feel the thick slime of desire crawling all over me? Smothering me with the hot night? Their bare chests cooled, a scarf of air brushed my legs. I pulled off the damp cotton, glanced quickly at Cliff and lay down stiff next to Peter. Purring tape whirring fast, a thud, motor still straining before it clicked off. Only the frogs now. And our bodies ticking, cooling like engines, radiators contracting. Our heat seeped slowly into the night air, maybe even up into the stars. Skin tightened and tingled. Cliff shifted on the table.

'There's space here, you know.'

'Na man, I cool.'

But without looking across, he sat up, came over and

lay down gently on the mattress next to me. Not touching, holding his body together, tense.

'Got enough space?' Peter asking.

We shuffled across, he inched closer, relaxing slightly. Arm on my side tucked up under his head, hip and leg running along mine, the top of my arm met the cool smooth skin of his chest. I could feel his breaths, cautious as mine, pushing at his ribs, each puff held. Peter's hand stirred on my stomach, it felt different.

A melting kiss. Slowly. Eyes flashing, a face flicking away and then coming closer. Hands meeting suddenly. Another hand searching, raising quicksilver blood. Nipples waiting, wanting. None of us could see the stars. The night and silent trees crept closer. Silky skin and lips moistening, sliding. Eyelash wings and pulses fanning. The soft air released us, turned us and pressed us. None of us could see the stars.

* * *

Next morning after breakfast, Oliver off to school, Peter and I sat at our desks keeping our secrets like children, waiting for the headmaster to find out. The mixture of sticky syrup skin, tested love and stretched boundaries hid in my mouth like a stolen sweet. It made us gentle with each other, extra nice to Oliver, busy, waiting to find a quiet spot to bare our new bond.

Cliff called again. The delayed click of the payphone signalling ahead.

'Yeah. I ain' doing nuthing. Just cool.'

Jumped a panic into my throat, unprepared to face the night again so soon. Too quickly, he arrived at the gate, came crunching in, the gravel path theme song of the house. Brought night and skin in with him. Skin that you could see now in the day. Smiles, shyness, a shared locket. He too.

'You okay?'

'I cool.' Eyes flashing away, came back, rested a little longer. Voice stronger.

'What you want to do? We're in the study till three.'

'You still have de movie?' A faint embarrassment in his tone, a boyness in the way he took off his cap and shoes and followed me to the spare room. Set himself on the edge of the bed and turned the volume down low. The silver bus started driving again.

Peter looked up as I returned to the study next door. 'What's he doing?'

'Getting on the bus!'

We both laughed, half wondering, remembering the depressing struggle the fella put up, effing this and effing that, trying to gain some dignity. Shouldn't we talk to Cliff about last night? But what to say? Don't know myself, hardly even know him. Our backs to each other, half attending to what had to be done on our desks.

'God, I take for ever to write a fax!'

'He really wants to look at that film again?'

'I guess he doesn't know what else to do.'

De star-boy, Leon, watching me with he face angry same way. Just come out'a jail, and he father blocking he. Refuse to meet he father eye. Dat same father who was never dere for he. Leon turn and we eye lock.

'Love you,' I said to Peter's back.

He stopped and turned round, grinning. 'What! With all the sexy ruderies and carrying-on?'

'I love you more.' Was the strangest thing a body could feel, but true. 'With all them carrying-ons, I do.'

'Ha!' Stretched out his chin and kissed my forehead. 'My Dou. You liked it well enough though! You should see yourself. Excited! You had me worried there for a minute!'

'I can't believe what we've done! You realise it? I'm a decent parent, you know!'

'Who, you? You must be joking! What you mean, anyway, we're all consenting adults, aren't we?'

'God knows what Cliff has made of it.'

We had laid awake last night trying not to talk about it. To understand the desire. Was it a need? Why not jealousy instead of excitement? Holding each other, passion growing secretly. Possessiveness heightening our own lust. Unexplainable intensified love to express.

'But we don't need that? We have enough sex as it is! You don't give me a break, Peter!'

'We don't *need* it, but that don't mean you're blind to attractive people, does it? You're attracted to him, aren't you.'

'Nmn . . .'

'Come on, you find him very attractive, right?'

'Yes. He has a really beautiful body. And I think he's a nice person.'

'Well you think *he* didn't find it enjoyable? He wasn't shy then.'

'You think he'll tell Ossi?'

'No idea. You can't tell what he's thinking when he's trying so hard to be cool.'

'Shy.'

'He's the one who said Ossi likes to talk about people's business, Bella. Maybe he won't tell him. Cliff seems to be the sensitive one. It's so hard to have a conversation with him though, his accent's really heavy. Why? You worried?'

'Yes! He might spread it all over Plymuth. His own version. You just can't tell.'

But Peter seemed to trust him somehow. He didn't even think Ossi could be deliberately malicious. Trusting them at face value. Making me feel like the devious mind.

'Well?'

'Well I don't know. Don't know . . .'

But on top of everything else, a tenderness for this man Peter welled up inside me. Flowed slow as molasses into my toes and my fingers trying to type my letters, all to the tip of my nose, the glands in my throat.

'Love you.' Couldn't describe it no other way. Felt then like I'd felt plenty times before, that I could see why people end up saying the same cliché love words over and over again. Wasn't no new words to describe it, something old as man, warming as food. Now melded with all kinds of things. Things I never dared dream of.

Watch me nuh, here in dis room. The stylie doorway frame outside like one'a Bella pi'tures. Sun bouncing coming in on de blue floor, jamming the foot of a old-time curly chair and them colour-colour cushions. Four bedpost posing round me, design like a crown. Watch me nuh. Leon is a stupid fella. He go to get ketch. Trying to get away and run through suck-sand swamp, wit' handcuffs on. I would'a never do dat. The old fellas trying to make him go on a march. A million black man. Leon watching me wit' he broad nose flaying. A ugly fella, en't? Bussing he tuck to get away. Frighten like hell! I just cool. De stupid fella get ketch. He go have to go back in jail.

Watching me hard. I watch he back from the side'a me eye. Put up me foot on the bed, the ceiling fan scratching over me head. Peeta an' dem must'e almost finish next door.

* * *

We all went to pick up Oliver from school. He climbed in the back with Cliff. 'Hello, Cool Dude.'

'Hi, Small Man.'

A short spin in the car back to home, Cliff slung low on the back seat, Oliver relating his day and watching him all the time. At home, Oliver wanted to watch his video. *Treasure Island* with The Muppets. Cliff headed for the spare room again. Hoots came shooting out of the room. Oliver's kya-kya-kyes, Cliff's whea'a and ayes. Had a good time, the two of them. Knee-slapping, dribble-laughing good time.

'Whoo boy, da' flim real good. I like Whadever. Any-thing you say, he just say "Whadever". Yeah boy!'

'That's all he says, "Whadever"! You ever see *Space Jam?*'

'Da's the one wit' Michael Jordan and dem cartoon fellas. Yeah, I like dat movie boy! I watch it four time already and I could watch it again.'

'You want to play on my computer?'

'Umn . . . whadever.'

Hunching over laughing, Oliver watching me and laughing, 'whadever' kya-kya-kyaing, they went into Oliver's room. Cliff's face relaxing clean, more comfortable with himself. Oliver trying to show him how to do the sailing program. He fiddling with the toys on the desk. Till dinner time.

'Cliff, what you want to drink?'

'Whadever! Aye . . . da' t'ing is real kicks boy. Whadever.'

'You'd like some more fish?'

He and Oliver whadever'ed together and cracked up laughing.

'Looks like you found a friend, Oliver.'

Time Together

He eased into our lives. Ossi came too sometimes, bounced round the place full of beans. Helping to cook, running on the treadmill, falling off laughing. Crashing asleep like a puppy. They shed their twinness as colts change coat, two shiny young adults emerging, proud in brotherhood but a spirit apart. Ossi noticed it, Cliff's new mystery, searched for the source but was soon bored. Like with the quiet dinners and domestic routine. 'Allyou doesn' get boring wit' dis easy-easy life?'

Cliff stayed, opening up, relaxing from cool, trying to communicate. Driving around with us grocery-shopping, going for swims. Peter took him sailing. After Oliver's turn, he climbed on, crouching up like Peter, them balancing the tipply dinghy. Leaning back, bracing out against the wind, Cliff looking at Peter steering them out. The wind that day gave them a gusty ride. Toppled them over, whisked them off again. They came back in tired and beaming, sunset water behind them, with a boy-to-man closeness. Held it in the water drops in their hair, in their hands passing a rope, in their smiles at themselves. An almost embarrassingly simple pleasure, being beat-up by the sea. Raised a pride in me to see such a thing. Something shared by people so different, a similarity so human and fine. One of these things that make ordinary people beautiful and beauty exquisite. So joyous could make me sing. Every time I glimpsed this hidden soft feather in

Cliff's breast, my faith in life grew. Grew an admiration for Cliff that jostled My Dou's love, jumbled desire?

Cliff danced the 'black dallie' around. Smack-kissed its cheek, compared abs, grinning, 'De body well cut, eh?' Imitating its pose in the shower. Soaping and laughing. Arms snaking me, cupping. Waist pressing me against Peter.

'Whoy! Dat's a big one for a white man, Peeta!'

'How would you know!'

Mixing up time and bodies didn't seem to affect Cliff or Peter. Maybe it's me worrying about things that don't exist. Or men's refusal to look into emotion's eyeholes.

The two of them squeezed together, hip to hip, same height.

'Look, 'e same size eh? You good, yes!'

*   *   *

Other times too. Stripping off, sharing towels, changing on hot sand in front of each other. Back Bay sun blazing our skin smooth, goose-bumps in the cold blue-green water, toes sinking into coarse sand, water patterns snaking over magnified skin. We rolled in the time we spent together. Romped and splashed around in it. Touched faces, exchanged glimpses, each imagining what we wanted. Flirting with newness, different roles. Romantic postures, not thinking of what really couldn't happen. Nobody demanded, nobody expected. Whadever. The days shifted shape like sand and we walked softly on it.

But it wasn't new that we walked on fresh wet sand and watched the water run from the weight of our feet. Peter worked hard. Harder than I ever could. Slogging away at problems for hours on screen. Flying all over the world to meet and listen, present, solve. At first I thought his brusqueness was business arrogance. Till I saw the worry eat at him while he worked, the frustrations with his clients and with the system in which he had to figure out the solution. We'd talk about his work for hours, him explaining the legal terms, understanding better himself by explaining to me. My work never tested my brain like that. Through long discussions, arguments and theories, my insecurities about education faded. Fierce logic opened my mouth.

The same likes in music, even. First time Peter dug up his old Eddy Grant and Fela Kuti tapes it sprung the gladness into my heart again. And art and films and books. Even furniture, fabrics and clothes. Same sand we walking on. The difference in our backgrounds – he just post-war England, me post-hippy Caribbean, he looking like a stylish brusque businessman at first glance, me like some Unicef Third World child – the differences and sameness made us walk softly on that sand. We played with it. Scooped big handfuls, covered our legs, buried each other, rubbed it in our hair. Grew bold together, like children. Knowing it could wash away. Could wash away from right under you.

And even after I gave birth to our child, made of both our blood and watched him grow in his own way, that only made time seem shorter, years fly faster and Oliver daily proof that you can't hold a living thing back, or mould it, no matter how much you love. And our living thing is love. Can't rule it and tame it, separate it and chain it. A living thing by itself.

Me Mind Far

Me and Ossi out on the jetty and I set down on the old pump base. He li'l friends and them always around. Four big Plymuth women sitting at the end old-talking and breezing. A cool afternoon, sky cast-over but no rain go fall. Water smooth and me mind far.

Them boys jump in. They does watch me different now. Nuff respect. Jumping and checking to see I watching. As if I never know them. Like I have a car and they want a ride. But I ain' taking them on. Baby Keisha face picture in me mind. Is a while I ain' hoist she up on me head. One'a them boys jump and splash some water by a woman.

'Aye boy! Don' play yuh li'l effing tail by me, yuh-know!'

The boy laughing and skinning he bumsey for she, Ossi stand-up watching and holding he mouth.

'Boy, you ain' shame'a yuh nasty black ass?' Steups. 'Yuh mudda neva teach you no mannars?'

The other lady tell she, 'Don' bother with dem so. All like he far-gone.' Turn and give me and Ossi a cut-eye.

Far-gone, nuh. Far as me mind. No words couldn'a reach. No feelings can't reach there neither. Was a thing I couldn'a think 'bout too long. It more like a jellyfish – what dem people loose out in me. Bella. One minute, you see it in the water moving, hanging so, next minute you see it cam'aflage gone. It there yuh-know, but you just can't

86

see it. Pretty as it be, it gone. One with the water. And then when you take it out'a the water how it does look? Wither up, ugly and out'a place. I can't study that nuh. Some things doesn' be to understand. As it come, is so it is. Far-gone the women them say, yes.

Ossi see me mind far. He looking to open he mouth but he don't say nuthing. Them women grumbling. One raise she big bambazam off the box she was setting on and slap the old pump. 'Plymuth people too dotish!'

'Eh-heh.'

'You ain' see how dem young boy so stupid and igna-rant? Anything people put there for dem, they mash-up. Phone box, they mash it up. Standpipe, they mash-up. A dotish set'a people!'

'Stupid and ignarant black people, nuh.'

Ossi hetch he pants and drag on he slippers. Start slapsing he way up the jetty turning he head, waiting for me to follow.

We go we way up the jetty, heading home. Them boys still there ramping and cravorting in the water.

'I only hope you know what it is yuh doing,' Ossi say and peeping to see me face as we walking. 'You think you could handle yuhself?'

I ain' telling he nuthing. I does can't hold-back meself. But I could handle meself. Sweet sexing skin and Peter only encouraging. How a man could do that, boy? He own wife. Me and another fella sex a girl same-time already, we was just ketching a t'ing but this is the man own woman. And is not to say he don't love she, you could see it in he eye. He ain' shame to tell she he love she right in front'a me. I never see people so. Sexing up and down and loving each another so. I couldn'a able with that, nuh. I just like how he is though, Peeta. He don't watch he mouth for nobody and he ain' checking on people.

Ossi still walking 'longside, watching me now and again. I still don't tell him nuthing. Watch some'a Tomo fellas now. Check how Dobermann and Jukie watching me, eh. Different, en't? Watching me, head rake-back, holding me in they eyes. Like I just join them. Like I must'e selling fucking dope. Nobody don't know nuthing but they there thinking what the hell they want to think, talking what the hell they want to say. Whadever, what the fuck, eh.

Soon as we reach in the porch Lynette start. 'Is only when day done allyou reaching here. Coming from whey-ever it is you was roaming. Now allyou coming looking for food to eat. Well it have none! It have no food in de house and I ain' cook not a drop!'

Baby Keisha set down without a panty on the floor, vest dirty and she hair ain' comb. 'Clee!' she call me, smile and set back she face strict to the envelope she struggling to open.

Ossi throw heself down in a chair. 'Whoy!'

'Whoy? Is work you was working so hard today make you tired so, whoy? De sheep still ain' bring-in yet.'

Dirty cups and baby bottle on the kitchen counter top. A fly land on the rubber nipple.

'Where allyou come from now?'

Nobody don't answer she.

'Allyou ain' care with nobody? I talking to you!' shouting at Ossi.

'Gyal, wha' you'a get-on so for? Wha' happen?'

'You ain' see wha' happenin'?' She broad nose flare out. 'Yuh mudda bussing she tail out there and you just roaming. Now you coming looking fuh food.'

She can't see she isn't we mudda? Why the ass she can't see 'bout sheself and done. She must'e don't even know who Keisha fadda is. And she playing t'ing with sheself. Staying in the house trying to hide she business, when she is married-man keeper. Keisha could be a horner-child and all. Getting on as if she is me mudda.

'Watch me boy! . . .'

Me meself don't even know where Mudda is right about now. In Scarbro. Fighting-up with goods or by the market. Smoking she li'l cigritte. Any kind'a work she get she does do. Construction work, road work when she ketch it. Mudda ain' easy.

'Whey Mudda?' Ossi akse and Lynette swing round.

'You aksing me whey de fuck Mudda is? KEISHA!'

Keisha rip open the envelope before Lynette jump on she, lift she up by one hand and start giving she lash. Keisha screaming and spin round, she arm twist.

'What de hell you have to knock de child so?' I bawl out.

'Eh?' She drop Keisha. 'Who you t'ink you is – a man? Don' forget yuhself with me, Cliff.'

'Hush yuh mouth!'

'I ain' hushing my mouth! You think because you reach in big house you big. You is a big-man now, eh? Well I know you and yuh nasty ways, yuh li'l t—'

I give she one slap and she fly. Ossi eye open big and Keisha stop cry. The hell she ain' me mudda and I ain' go take no mouth from she! Slam the porch door and go down the road, blood riling in me.

Dese Young Fellas

Thomas and Oliver treated the spare room like it was Cliff's, the video always on once he was there. But the respect eased along still – the telephone call before coming, not taking the liberty of helping himself from the fridge, understanding if we said we were busy. The only thing we couldn't understand was the lack of ambition. Thomas and me'd wonder, try to figure out how come. The 'mudda'? No father? What?

' "Cooling" is Cliff's occupation, Thomas. A bit of fishing when he feels like it.'

One of our long talks in the middle of clearing the table, Thomas mop in hand and me towel-clad on my way to the bathroom. Long circular talks, always coming back to the same things – how come, why?

Thomas's old-time manners reminded me of my childhood. The village life and struggle he'd gone through wasn't far from Cliff's background – broken home, not having much, dropping out of school – but he still couldn't understand the attitude today. His gentle worry and manners made people see him as old-timish and soft. To me he was wise beyond his thirty-five years. Trini-red, they called him, like Brian Lara and from the Santa Cruz valley too. Broad back, broad features, a generous ready smile and eyes that couldn't hide a doubt.

'Girl,' he put the teapot onto the tray, 'dese young

fellas, dat is how they is dese days. It have plenty like him don' want to do nuthing.' Turned down his mouth.

'But he used to work in a dive shop – and hear what happened then: they asked him to clean the toilet. Not him alone, mind you, others had to take turns cleaning the staff toilet and equipment shed. You know what he told them? "Cleaning toilet? I ain' cleaning nobody shit". He said, "Dem hire me fuh help on de boat and assis' tourist and t'ing".'

Thomas already shaking his head. 'And what about if he was to go New York? You don' think he would do janitor work there? You go see how fast he cleaning! Look at them big house here now, them people who come back from foreign and build here. You know what kind'a work some'a them had to do.'

'But that's different, Thomas, people would do anything when they reach over there. Not here though.'

'Dat is them. And dat is why I always say, when you see people have they things, you can't jealous, 'cause you don' know how hard they had to work to get it.'

'It's not that there's no work to do, you-know Thomas, Cliff just wants to "chill". Whole day, he looking for a way to "chill". The cycle shop doesn't pay much and he says "goverment don' have no more ten-days work", so that is it.'

'I know. But dese young fellas want de nice clothes, "speakers, sneakers and earring". But they don' want to work. And you can't tell dem a t'ing! At least dis one don' have attitude. At least he mudda teach he some manners. He say he go fix me cycle.'

'I hope he asks you to borrow it.'

'Yeah, yeah. Heh, except for the first time.' Thomas smiled, still embarrassed about the incident. Cliff took the bike without asking. He and Ossi figured Thomas wasn't a relative, must be a yardboy, were looking to treat him how they think one should be treated. That was the only time we had to put Cliff straight – and Thomas wouldn't even have told me if I hadn't asked. I knew from his eyes that he didn't trust Cliff and Ossi, didn't approve of us being so trusting with them but he'd never let his way come before ours.

'According to them construction work is "slave wo'k", Thomas. Working in hotel is "slave wo'k". Fishing's too hard, too much hot sun. Farming is "old-time wo'k". Listen, in Immortelle Valley Restaurant the other day, a young waiter stood up – in front of women working there and the customers – he said, "I can get more money on the street". He means hustling tourist women! When a woman asked him if he ain' shame, he said, "No. Is money". Standing up bold-face saying that!'

'But they doesn't have no shame dese days. The way my mother bring me up, if you don' have, you go wit'out. A man can't go and akse a woman fuh money. Dat's embarrassing! And yet I tired seeing dat happen now. And ignarant yuh-know, some'a them fellas real ignarant. Rememba dat AIDS lady in de papers?'

'Oh yes! She was from Switzerland or somewhere . . .'

The HIV-positive woman had slept with about eleven men in two weeks in Tobago before the police locked her up, tried to charge her but ended up deporting her.

'But de woman say in court that she have a card saying dat she is HIV, and she does always show it to a man before they have sex. De card was print-up in de newspapers, it had a photo and HIV mark up clear. She say it was they choice, she didn' trick nobody.'

'Yes, I remember all the fuss in the paper ... "nasty tourist women" and such.'

'But de shameful t'ing is, Bella, when dey akse de fellas if they know she was infected, some'a dem don' even know what HIV is! In dis day and age? How you could be living here and you ain' seeing, you ain' hearing ... wha' happen?'

'Maybe they don't want to know.'

'Ignarant, man! One fella say 'bout how, if he bathe wit' blue-soap and Clorox after, he can't get it. Another one say he does drink lime-water. Fellas t'ink they could get some obeah cure from de fixer-woman ...' Thomas's face was honestly puzzled. One of the many questions that floated through our house, lodging when they want to. An answer he searched for while watering the garden. Peter and I'd grow them, stretch them. Then they'd burst, a popped bubble, leaving you clutching at nothing. Thomas knew, though, that some things just couldn't be explained, that's how he lived his life. He watched and weighed with tradition. It showed every day in measured movements, a cautious brow.

'But what dese young fellas want to do?' Thomas asked me.

I couldn't guess any more than he could. 'Who knows, Thomas. I think this one might be able to keep himself out of trouble.'

* * *

In the darkroom with half-made images and cool chemical air, processing prints, preparing for my first exhibition. The scenes of the boats and markets in Cambodia, dense and colourful as they were, seemed to hold none of the life I'd seen there. The clear history in how a woman lifts a basket or ties a bundle of greens, what these people had gone through, every last family and how they carry it now in dusty smiles and quick eyes – none of that was caught. The lens had filtered it out, left it behind. The prints didn't make any sense. Even the local Tobago scenes – boats and fishing – slipped through the sieve. No links. No images of the rich language, the sway of it. Invisible undercurrents I've tried and tried to catch. The complexity of life, isolated on an island. The intensity of it, magnified sins and honesty changing colour before your eyes. Overwhelming and irrational, impossible to show.

All together in the living room later, projecting some slides, clicking past the weak images, looking for something I wanted to find.

'Da' is whey?' Cliff asked.

'Charlotteville.'

He laughed at the fisherman's hands. 'Wha', dey rough-looking boy!' Excited at a recognisable fruit. 'Da's, what you call it . . . wha' de 'ting name . . .'

Oliver pressed the button, commentary running. Peter teddy-soft with pride. And the crux of the illusion lay around me, dressed in changing images, different voices and norms.

De Black Dallie

We arrived at Hilda Schmitz's gate to show Cliff who'd made 'de black dallie'. She came out wiping her hands, eyes beaming.

'Oh my g'sh! Look who's here!'

Bending down to kiss her.

'Oh g'sh, you didn't tell me you were coming and now I am all sweaty and dirty, look at me.' Her eyes sparkling up at Cliff, then down at Oliver. 'Look at you! You growing. You rememba my dogs? And who's this gorgeous young man you have with you, eh?' Shining from my face to Peter's to Cliff's. 'Knockout. Real good-looking.'

Cliff's eyes and smile down by his feet.

'You know that, eh? But you're all good-looking, come in, come in. We have to go around because these steps not finished yet.'

'You're looking really well too, Hilda.'

She did too, even sweaty and smeared with sawdust and charcoal. Lipstick always bright red, wispy blonde hair piled up in a bun with woollen yarn woven in. Her whole stockiness, square shoulders and handsome face had a strong Germanic farm-girl beauty; I could see her in an Alpine meadow. But she was at home here, here in this heat, singing along in her Tobago-German accent. We followed, towering over her, gaping at the amazing façade of her studio and chapel.

'It's looking great!'

Knobs and curves, concrete details and columns in relief stretched along the front, hiding the whole of her old gingerbread wooden house. In each playful classical panel she had started drawing and painting images – Medusa, Adam and Eve. A particular angel stuck out over the metal door. On the roof, sculpted birds, boobies and pelicans perched between white cones and balls, dogs with tails straight out. Above us in a corner alcove, a cast bronze of *Little Black Boy* stood watching, a multi-coloured dance-skin painted on him. A workman moved high up against the blue sky.

'You like it?' She pointed at the façade. 'It never going to finish. Right, Winston? I said, it never going to finish!' Shouting up to the man. 'That's tha best mason. He from Moriah. All my workmen come from tha country, far, fah.' She turned to look again at Cliff. 'The workmen from around here lazy. And trouble!'

Peter mmn'd. 'I'm sure you know all about these things, Hilda.'

'Look, your black dolly up there.' I pointed him out to Cliff.

'Is de same one?'

'How he painted up so?' Oliver asked, squinting up at the colourful costume.

'What, baby? Oh, I just put some clothes on him. Come this way.'

We went down into her courtyard workshop, gazing up at her chapel. It stood on pillars, high slot windows, a robust façade with an arched metal door.

'Is that your boudoir, Hilda? You've done a lot since we've last been here.'

Charcoal sketches on the bare walls of the courtyard marked its creation, the ideal structure raised and erased.

'Boudoir? No. Oh, yes, I sleep there. It's the only place that's secure. Me alone here, you know. When night comes I go up there and lock tha door. But that will be my studio, come and see . . . See? A good space, eh? Look out tha windows. I make them just my height to look out and all you can see is tha treetops and tha sea. No crap. Look all these ugly houses and things around. When I moved here there was none of that.'

We bent knees to try out the windows.

'Now my neighbours, they don't like me, they give me trouble for my outside toilet.'

'Yes?'

'Yes! They don't want these things round here, you see. But it doesn't smell.'

'A latrine,' I said to Cliff, just to see his disbelief and embarrassment. He couldn't hide it. How could a white woman have a latrine?

'Yes. Toilet and bath should be outside. Natural. No hat water. I always bathe with dipping. Cold water, no shower.'

Back in the courtyard workshop, half-born bodies of wood loomed everywhere. Ten-foot dancing people sketched on flat rough planks stacked along the wall. Broad shoulders at jaunty angles, huge hands, hats and full-lipped smiles. Real back-in-times people. Charcoal, chalk and remnants of green poison on wood the colour of mulatto skin. A gentle-smile woman, head tipped slightly, stood next to a tall man doing the jig. Her skirt hadn't come out of the tree trunk yet. Chains wrapped around her waist and chest suspended her from the rafters of the high-pitched tin roof.

'That's Wanda.'

'Her face is lovely just as it is.'

Bits of newspaper, a chainsaw and huge chisels, paint tins, wooden mallets, brushes and turpentine jars, jumbled up with sawdust and woodchips all around. A child emerging from the oak lump by the door. A ballerina. Cliff saw his face reflected in wood. I saw his eyes searching for more half-hewn familiar features.

'Olivah look, I have a snake living here. Up in the corner so.'

'Where, where? What kind of snake? How long?'

She lifted him up onto a block in the dim corner, smiling with me in celebration of his curiosity. 'Shush. He don't like to see noise.'

We quietly closed in behind Oliver, straining to see the dark dusty gap up in the rafters. The little pointed head set there under a slim coil, barely visible.

'How long is it?' Oliver whispered. 'Cliff, come and see.'

But Cliff hung back with his half-born people.

'Come and let's have a drink. I don't usually drink just yet but it's almost four a'clock. No, don't play with that dog Olivah, that's Peppa, she's getting very old and pesky.' She scrummaged round in her kitchen, shouting out. 'I save it up. I work hard. Hard I tell you, all day. Hot. Oh g'sh is hot and I dream, I dream of a nice cold beer. Cold, cole bee-ah. I can't wait for this nice cole bee-ah. At four a'clock every day I go down to Mount Irvine beach and . . . aahh. So good! And cold! But I have no beer here so you drink some rum. Is good for you. I have no refrigerator, so no cole bee-ah.'

'Come, come Hilda, surely you can afford a fridge.' Peter winked at her. 'Even a poor artist like you. How much do you sell your work for now, anyway?'

'No, no, no. I tell you. Recently I had to buy this

thing.' She pointed to it right behind us. A small washing machine. 'I couldn't take it no more, all this scrubbing. I getting old, you know. Look, more rum. I have soup, you want soup, baby? I couldn't do all this washing all tha time. Now, easy, I just put . . .'

'You need an agent, Hilda. You should be doing very well.'

Her frank face squinted at Peter with a mixture of fondness and amusement.

'Your work is good. Do you sell much in New York?'

'Not so much. I go there. I have good friends there. But you know they say an artist's work is never valuable till they ah dead.'

'Who says so?'

'Everybody knows. And then, when I die, then tha value is good.'

Both their eyes twinkling. She watched Oliver finish his soup and go back to tickling her stunted three-legged dog. Admiring everything about Oliver: 'I don't like children – but this one? Oh! He can come here any time, so sensitive and bright! His eyes, oh.' Whenever she looked at him she always looked to me in happy wonder. Look what you made! As she looks at another artist whose work she likes. Always made me beam stupidly in return, trying to tone it down to a modest maternal smirk.

Cliff was staring at the strange walls of the small struc-ture set away from the house.

'That's her bathroom.' I couldn't keep from looking either, at the precise blue silhouettes of men's bodies painted on the white walls. An arm outstretched. Shorts on.

'How she paint dem so?' He whispered to me but she heard.

'Tha workmen. I catch them and hold them against the wall, then paint, hah!'

The balls of this woman. More balls than I've ever seen. More than any of the big hulking men macho-ing themselves around. She'd been in Tobago twentysomething years now, spending semesters teaching sculpture at a university in Germany. Going for her bee-ah at Mount Irvine Public Beach Facility, every day. Dancing Sunday nights into Monday mornings at Sunday School in Buccoo village. Telling me, 'You have to go *after* midnight, that's when all the tourists go home. Then, tha blacker it gets tha better. Movements. You know?' Painting up the Anglican church in Black Rock with brown saints, *Creation of Adam* after William Blake. Capturing faces, postures and dances in cured wood. This ballsy German woman chiselling handsome black people, is Tobago's resident artist. And people come from Trinidad and don't bother to visit her studio. 'Dat white woman lusting after black man. We all know why she living in Tobago, so she could get plenty. And Tobagonians so stupid, they like dat. Look how she does make dem look, with bumsey cock-out and big broad nose'. And others visit her studio with new money because she is a 'real international artist', teaching at a real university in Europe, her work admired by Trinidadian artists and intellectuals. They visit her Tobago museum with handbags and holiday sandals. 'Nigel, look at dat one there. It luvely, eh? You know what I seeing? A fish. It look like a fish'. Giggling and snickering at the phallus relief, trying hard to admire the African – but not 'back to Africa' – gazes from the suave features crowding the studio. A few want to buy, maybe as proof of their artistic taste, a cut above the average middle class. But Hilda watches them all, through and through. Stone-facing the oohs and aahs, kindling those she likes. Looking for 'real' people, eccentrics she can relate to, homes for her offspring.

'But Peter, I don't want them to go all over tha place in cold countries, in some stupid living room. No! At all! It's not right.' Turning to Cliff. 'So anyway. You. What's your name? Whey you from? Tell me.'

'Me? Cliff. From Plymouth.'

'From Plymouth? Whaat. That is a bad place. You know that, eh? I could live anywhere in Tobago but not in Plymouth.'

'What you mean?' Peter asked, knowing full well.

'You know eh?' Chucked her chin at Cliff, he looking down smiling. 'Drugs. Too much drugs there. Right?'

'Un-huhn. It have drugs dere in true.'

'I hope you not in that, eh! Or else I don't want to see you round these people.'

'Me? Na! Un-unh, I not in dat, man.' Laughed to himself.

'You don't look like that. Awright.' Gave him another once-over.

'What happened to the young man you had here Hilda?'

'Ribs? He not here any more. He kept going down, down. First he put his hair in locks, you know, pretty-pretty. And then he start in this tourist racket, doing all kind of women. And he don't care! I bring suitcases of condoms, plenty. And he stupid, no words. Getting on my nerbes. He don't even want to try to learn few-few words like a baby! Can't speak proper but admiring himself all the time. He was getting on my nerbes, I tell you.'

'But he was nice eh, Hilda, you never had him?'

'No! No, no, I finish with sex long time now. Anyway

he useless in bed, everybody know, too lazy. When he start with tha marijuana thing, I tell him one-time, out. So now is me alone.'

Cliff's eyes opened big, mouth straight, half frightened of this woman.

Hilda glared at him. 'You too good-looking. You know that?' She chinned a smile at his giggle and we sipped from the small heavy glasses. The fire rum burned our throats, opened up our bellies and Peter stretched out. Oliver was digging round the side of the house with the dogs. I nodded to Cliff, rose and took him to see the rest of Hilda's family inside the studio.

We entered the vault, two stories high, cool and dim. A towering, embracing brown *Jesus* leaned against the bay windows, reaching all the way up to the roof with pelicans diving and animals climbing in the folds of his robes. The whites of Ribs's eyes stared from his blue naked body, relief against orange. Thick flowers and leaf patterns, totees and love symbols from some Haitian god tried to disguise themselves against the walls. And looking on, looming, stretching over our shoulders, the tall people paused. Silent in the lofty room smelling of wood and paint and a faint trace of concrete powder.

'Da' woman make all dese?'

His voice rumbled round the room like his eyes, bumping from one figure to the next. Moving between them like a living one, dwarfed. Between torsos like Ossi's, elongated even more, hips askew. A woman like his mother in party clothes laughed with her head back, hands in the air. Another one, bumsey out, thick legs bent, feet apart, clapped her hands, wining to some music. A light-skin lady in coat and hat held a little dog up on her shoulder. A male dancer with high heels pointed his foot up, straight past his top hat. *La Diablesse* with her ruffled skirts and cow-hoof foot bent forward. An iguana clutched at *Papa Bois*'s thigh.

Downstairs, *The Wedding People* welcomed us, dressed up in suits, crowding and dancing, huge hands with gold rings, tight shoes fixed in place.

'Dey real good, eh? Dey look real. She good!'

'Yes, it's special.'

The scale and presence of all the dancing guests quieted us. The living barely moving in half-light, stirring specks of magic dust, could make anything happen. These moments are the images I want to capture. The rare glimpses through objects and people, through the worn layer of everyday living, to something more exquisite. Had Cliff seen it too? He sucked in his belly and we pushed out into the bright light. Wanda smiled knowingly as we passed her again.

'I like them unfinished, though.'

'Uh. You can see dem more live, en't?'

* * *

Smooth smooth skin. Eyes meeting. Teeth clashing in sudden kisses. A hand. Whose hand? Do you want him to touch me there? Stroking, guiding. A back arched. Long leg muscles taut, belly stretched. Curves of tight skin moving, sliding. I want you. Fingers pressing tight. Gripping. Like this? Breasts held, licked. Tongues. All everywhere, I want. Smooth smooth skin, sinews swelling. Seizing. Slowly. Blood comes back to my pupils and I can see straight into Peter's. My Dou. We held tight and rocked. Checking each other's eyes. My Dou.

History Walking

Driving through the green shady bamboo corner, past the quiet grassy hills, the pin-up cow and squiggly coconut tree to Immortelle Valley Restaurant for Saturday lunch – Peter and I, Oliver and his friend. The little river, stream really, ran through cocoa trees across the front of the open deck, under a bridge by towering bamboo, papyrus, wild dasheen and red cat-tails rippling down the banks. All the air mottled green in the day. Alive black ink in the night, beyond the yellow lights.

Sat at our corner table and took off our shoes. The boys headed for the pool where the crayfish crawled. Peter'd been quiet all morning. Talking to me but his eyes had dead patches in them. The sour-faced lady came to take our orders and long before our salads came I knew he wouldn't voice it. But the cold patches broke into little irritated comments. Swatting.

'You're not feeling insecure about us, are you?'

'What! Of course not! Although it wouldn't be surprising if I was, seeing how you behave! You should see yourself! You really want him, don't you?'

'Dou, if there's any doubt, it's not worth it. There's no doubt in everything I have for you. And I would never do this without you.'

'It doesn't look like it sometimes. You get so carried away, I might as well not be there.'

'Okay, okay, maybe just once or twice that's happened.

But I can't control it. And you want it too. You want to see me excited but not carried away?'

'It's not the excitement, it's when you exclude me. Your naive romance for his rootsy background or something.'

'What? Because I can understand what Cliff's saying? Because I can talk his language?' Hadn't even thought about it. Sharing a piece of identity with Cliff never occurred to me as something that excluded Peter. A separate thing from sex and love: friendship. Maybe the only thing that was just between Cliff and me.

'But my sexual attraction to him – to having both of you – must make you jealous. And that excites you, doesn't it? The danger. It tests you, us, there's a risk. Isn't that it? The thrill?'

'Of course! But it's for us, isn't it? What else do you want from Cliff? You think you're from his background? It's very nerve-racking for me at times.' His eyes turned down to his plate but we both knew the point his voice had reached.

My heart could've filled the empty plate in front of him. But I couldn't lump it out right here. 'I get frightened too, My Dou. Maybe . . .'

And if we're feeling like that, what the hell must be going through Cliff's mind? His responses seemed so mature, so sensitive to Peter, without competitiveness, they had wiped away my feelings of guilt that we may be corrupting him. Encouraging him to do things that were wrong, that he didn't like. We might have taken advantage. When I talked to Cliff about it, he laughed. 'Since I ten I been having sex, yuh-know. Da' ain' nuthing. I brush two gyal together a'ready. Don' feel no how, I ain' no li'l boy'. Cool and able to 'handle' himself. Macho-ing up on the outside, sensitive inside. Maybe more comfortable

with men, even though he had to struggle to communicate with Peter. I remembered their deep voices and
laughs.

'But what about you and Cliff, what was he trying to
tell you that first night in the kitchen?'

Peter's thoughts came round. 'Cliff? He was quite open
actually, he was trying to tell me about a girlfriend he
had, something about what he liked and what he didn't.'

'A man-to-man talk.'

'Except it was very hard to keep up with his heavy
dialect. But another time, just the other day, he asked me
if I would like him to find a girl for me.'

'What!'

'Yes. He's only had one girlfriend but he's had a lot of
sex. "Sexed plenty girls", according to him. He likes your
kind of looks. And then he was offering to find a nice
"red-skin" girl for me. Really.'

'You mean "on the side" for you, or what?'

'I don't know but I really had to convince him that I
wasn't interested in that kind of thing. That we're not like
that. He was serious too.'

'I can't believe . . . and you didn't even tell me. I guess
he must've seen it as being nice to you, man to man!'

'Or maybe he just thinks of us as a strange foreign
couple who have a lot of strange sex. Look at it from his
perspective, Bella.' A barb swung on the end of his words
but as soon as he saw me hurt, staring at it, he softened.
Every trace of ice melted from him. 'Maybe he meant a
girl to share! You might like that even more – with another
woman!'

'Ah! No! I don't know if I could handle that. But I'm
not against it!'

'Oh you're not, aren't you!'

'No. But you couldn't blame me if I'd be jealous . . .
'cause I'm younger than you and . . .'

'I'll give you younger, you . . .'

We filled-in back together. Closer, laughing. The crayfish torturers teased their prey with bits of bread, jerking
them straight out of the water. Excited shrieks bouncing
out with a river-echo clearness.

'I get a big one, I get a big one!'

'Leh me see, leh me see!'

Sitting under the huge old water wheel, 'McCormack,
Glasgow 1857' stamped in its black iron, a steam boiler,
remnants of mossy brick walls – history still lives here.
Elva, the waitress from Plymouth, came to clear the table,
back as straight, face as still as African ancestors. Her
proud silent walk took her past the chimney with its
crumbling top, past the sugar train of broken cast-iron
coppers, through the swing doors into the kitchen. Ragga-
soca music banging from a tinny radio, clattering around
in there. A young fella's huge shoulders moved to the
sink by the window. High-pitched laugh crackled with a
whooy! Elva sailed back out of the doors towards us, face
set the same way as when she went in.

'They having a party in there?'

A quirk caught the corner of her mouth, rolled her eyes
at the kitchen. 'Humf. Allyou ready for the bill?'

This land was an Amerindian settlement long before
sugar days. Now, struggling to be the best restaurant,
historic site and nature centre in Tobago. But the spirits
are still too close. Like in the rest of this beautiful island,
the bitter taste of slavery is in the earth itself, drawn up
by the trees into their leaves, a rot in the seed of their
fruit. A bile in people's minds. Now tourism is the trade,

the new crop. But still it brings people who have to be served, white people expecting something in return for the Yankee dollar. It feeds the politicians' egos, fattens their pockets, is regurgitated in public speeches, eagerly swallowed by voters, churned up with a sense of justice and angry pride, spiked with the bile.

George Antoine, the proprietor, came sauntering up to our table, smiling to himself as usual. We beamed back at him as you can't help doing, reflecting his smile.

'Good to see you, George. How's the sweltering metropolis of Port of Spain been treating you?'

'Well, not too bad yuh-know, not too bad. You know how it is. Keeping myself busy.'

He keeps smiling to himself when he's talking, looking at the table corners, under the edge of a napkin, as if there's some amusing detail hiding there. A short unassuming man, mixed with every race you could find in Trinidad, round-faced, twinkle-eyed, he could almost be Polynesian. He'd wander in and out of his establishment almost unnoticed, potter around in the garden, help with the mud oven, breeding and nursing his crayfish in the river.

'I see your restaurant's doing well, George. It was full again the other night.'

'Well, we trying. Little by little . . .' Still smiling, head twisted, sharing secrets with the lizard poised on the balisier leaf, some fallen immortelle flowers scattered on the bright green moss. '. . . Have to keep trying to improve the place.'

'Still the best restaurant in Tobago.'

'Well allyou should know the menu by heart!' A joke shared with us, with our eyes. And we shared it with all the staff, us turning up regularly, pretending to be new visitors. Even Elva smiled at our silly game.

'You should have some rooms here too. Nature, quiet, wilderness and all that, for the hairy-legs-and-sandals lot.'

'But the thing is, it's hard to get people to guard the place at night. They don't stay, they frightened! Dis thing with the jumbies and spirits in the area, is a problem . . .' Belly jumping with an inside laugh.

We couldn't be serious about it either. Everybody knew about the 'hauntings' of old estates, especially this one, so close to Les Coteaux. Foreigners laughed or became intrigued but locals ran.

'Serious, is a serious problem. You can't get security guards to stay here at night. We gone through all the companies that exist in Tobago! Nothing happens to them, but when you come in the morning, you meet them lock-up in the little box by the gate there, tight-tight so not a breeze could get in.'

Encouraged, his chuckles building up to a better joke.

'I never see nothing here to 'fraid. They tell me they hear all kind'a chains dragging and t'ing, but I never hear nothing. Look the other night, I couldn't sleep, I had just reach home late from some drinks thing at a hotel and I couldn't sleep, so I say let me pass round and check everything okay. Eh-eh, when I reach here, I park-up, I ain' see no guard. Well was two a'them on that night 'cause we figure it would help with the courage, yuh-know. And we have the dog that they supposed to loose in the night. I get out, I walk around, I still ain' see nobody. The dog not even around so I start calling now. Soon as I start calling, the dog start barking but it sounding like it lock-up. I find it strange. I calling and walking to go and check the office. I still ain' seeing no guards, no sign a'them nowhere. Eh! Then I realise the barking coming from the kitchen! Heh! Oh God, hee . . .'

Laughing in the best part of the joke.

'So I reach the kitchen door and I unlock it with me key. I pulling the door now, as I pull so . . . I feel the door pull back! Heh! The dog barking more, I pulling and the door pulling back. Is them guards inside'a there! They tie-up the door with a rope . . . hee . . . and holding on dear life!'

Us cracking up too, imagining.

'I call out, "Is me, is George!" but the dog barking more and they pulling more . . . Oh Lord! Look, I had to laugh yuh-know. All the time they was inside there, hearing me calling and thinking is jumbie. When they do realise is me and open the door, them big fellas real shake-up! You know they leave and say they ain' coming back? Oh Lord, you have to laugh yuh-know. Hee. What else you can do? You have to laugh in this place.'

That's what you have to do in these parts. Elva, folding napkins, smiled at George still giggling. In Trinidad too, you had to laugh at the politics, the crime, the bacchanal. This man's laugh lines and the smile in his eyes was what allowed him to walk together with history here.

'Where the boys? They catch out all my crayfish yet? There's a big mother one under a rock over so . . .'

We all went to search for the mother crayfish.

* * *

Peter had to go to Trinidad for a meeting next day. After dropping him off at the airport in the morning, a strange expectancy followed me through the house. If Cliff called and asked if he could come over – what? The tension stood behind me in the darkroom, breathing down on my conscience. If he came, would he behave different? Would I behave different? The question ran up the back of my leg. I waited but the call didn't come till afternoon, after school, when the day started cooling and relaxing into sunset. Ossi was with him. I picked them up from the cycle shop in Black Rock, Oliver with me, to go and meet Peter at the airport. The usual fellas and children outside the closed-up shack. A big woman with Spandex shorts stood opposite, bra top spanning her folds, a heavy arm draped on a fella with a big belly and big gold chain. A couple of young girls close by.

'Come! Is black man yuh want? Look, one here!'

Was only when I looked in the rear-view mirror I realised she was talking to me. Shouting out, slapping the man's shoulders, the girls round her hooting. I turned round to look, waiting for Ossi to get in.

'Yeah! Dis is real black man here. Don' worry wit' dem magger boys, come fuh de original t'ing!'

The man laughing a big gold-teeth laugh. Cliff's face mixing shame and shine, Ossi grinning, getting in the car and Oliver busy fiddling with the radio.

'Come! You can get certificate if yuh want. Look, black man here!'

Shouting out loud as we drove off. All of us laughing too. A certificate! Oh, Father balls in heaven! A certificate for tourists to take back home! Still couldn't believe it.

'Humpf, I ain' know na.' Ossi laughing his horsing laugh and slapping the outside of the car.

'What? What allyou laughing 'bout, Mum?'

'But I can't believe this woman! And look at the man! I couldn't pass that exam, you-know!'

'Da' is de owner'a de cycle shop. And da' is he woman. She does work dere sometimes.'

'You could get certificate for she too? Or she just catches tourists for him? Real black man! Oh father!'

We put on the Buju tape and cruised towards Crown Point. *Walk like a champion. Act like a champion. Gyal let me in, me gat de t'ing wha' you a wait 'pon.* High-pitched engines signalled the glint of Air Caribbean approaching low in the sky as we arrived. Ossi and Oliver running up the airport steps to watch it land, Cliff walking cool behind.

'It go touch just now! Watch, eh!' Ossi more excited than Oliver, squinting.

At the rail, the three of them waited for the tyres to bump, engines to roar, the man to signal with his orange sticks. Watched the plane turn and taxi towards us. A kind of wonder and thrill, some kind of pride to have witnessed such a thing filled all their three faces. Cliff and Ossi, legs braced against the rail, waiting, almost identical profiles, Oliver stretching up, his chin on the rail.

'My father's going to come out first. He always does.' Same witnessing pride in his little voice.

'I never went on one'a dem t'ing boy.' Ossi smacked his bottom lip and turned. 'I went Trinidad a'ready, but I went on de boat.'

He looked guilty of not having done, never been there. Looked down at his sneakers checking for mud but his admiring eye crept back to the silver plane. Cliff's smooth African mask was on quicker than a passing cloud, eyes slipping across to me before the lashed slits closed.

'I never been on the ferry.' Oliver tried to sympathise. 'Look, Dad!'

Ossi beamed and waved. Cliff even waved. Peter

flapped an arm at us, tie and hair flying, pants flapping in the breeze.

Folding himself into the front of the car, My Dou was smashing in his big white shirt and bright slanty-striped tie. Fresh, just walked out of Oxford or something like that, tousled-up, spectacled and bookish.

'Yuh look like a schoolboy Peeta! A office boy!'

He put on his John Lennon shades as we turned towards Pigeon Point. 'Ahh, that's better. Oh, God that flight was awful. Bumpy and sick-making. It was pouring with rain in Trinidad.'

'Yeah, it does make you feel sick, en't Peeta?'

'Awful.'

Pulled up by the fishing boats, Dr Piranha frantically gutting and filleting while the light lasted. Fresh snapper heaped on the scale-covered table, red in the glowing sun. A few fishermen slopping out their boats. An old woman sat on a cooler waiting for Piranha to finish cleaning her fish, mash-up wrinkly face taking in everything. She watched us arrive, two young fellas with black stick-legs, basketball vests and sneakers, a small boy heading for the water, a tall mix-blood woman and a clean-shirt white man with a tie.

'Office boy!' Cliff slapped Peter's shoulder.

The woman sucked her teeth loud – steups. Watched Cliff up and down. 'Office boy!' She muttered. 'Who he calling boy.' She cut-eye at his picky-ras hairstyle. Steups. 'Nasty good-fuh-nuthing. Can't even pass a comb in he hair. Sure he ain' have no wo'k neither. Good-fuh-nuthing. Who he calling boy?'

She looked to Peter like he should do something 'bout it but he hadn't heard her. Cliff wasn't taking her on. Ossi winked at me and beamed at her. 'Tantay!'

'Tantie who?' She steupsed again and turned away in disgust at what things had come to.

Golden syrup light folded warm waves on the sand. Piranha wasn't talking much today, working fast to beat the dark. Hands and scales flying, slicing quick, feeling for bones, fish eyes staring before being plopped in the bucket of bloody sea water. We watched, as the sun slipped away quietly and dark crept closer.

Back home, cooking the fish in the kitchen: 'When we going and see da' white lady again, eh Peeta?'

'Hilda?'

'Yeah. Da' woman kicksey, boy. Latrine, eh. First white woman I see have latrine. She don' care wit' nobody, nuh. She does do obeah?'

'Voodoo?' Peter seemed to have never even thought about her local reputation.

'De snake and dem t'ings she have mark-up. She could'a put a t'ing in de black dallie, boy.' Cliff looked at me. I didn't answer, could see that he didn't believe that either. 'We must go a next time, en't Peeta? But watch dis t'ing here . . .'

Now he needed help to fill in an application form for an ID card. Was a long time he had had to do this.

Office boy turned father. 'Well, what's the problem? Let's see. You *can* read, can't you?'

'Yeah, yeah. But is only one form I have, an' if I mess it up . . . and some a dem big word tie me up. It say a teacher or lawyer or a person of . . . have to sign. Look.'

Peter smoothed the soft grubby form onto the table. Inspected it while Cliff watched the top of his head.

'Okay. First name CLIFF. Last name DUNSTAN. Your mother's name before she married?'

'Dem ain' married nuh, me fadda and mudda. Is me

mudda name, Dunstan. I have a uncle in de force yuh-know.' Bent lower to catch Peter's eye. 'A corpral. Me fadda brudda. He does always akse Mudda 'bout me.'

'Sex? Too much!'

'No Peeta! En't they mean – man or woman, male 'r female? Heh. Too much?' Laughing like it's the best joke.

'Father's first name?'

'T'eodore. I ain' know how you spell dat nuh. He living up in country. I don' care with he. He have other chi'ren yuh-know, young young. You don' have no other chi'ren Peeta? You ain' want mo'? You could adop' me, yuh-know. Heh.'

Peter looked up from the form smiling his eyes up at Cliff. 'What? A big man like you?'

Ossi came slanting himself onto the kitchen bench. 'Who? Who is a big man? He?' Bounced Cliff out of his place. 'He just harden. But Peeta, you ain' want no harden, long-lengereh trouble like he. Is me is de younga one. I could l'arn still.'

'Yeah boy, he is a baby in true. Still sucking breast. And he like to drink plenty milk.'

'I tell you, breast is best, boy! Breast is best. Da wha' Mudda say. En't Peeta? You never hear yuh mudda say dat?'

I smiled to think of Peter's mother in Yorkshire even *thinking* about breastfeeding. Peter deprived, going looking for big full ones.

'Peter's never even seen his mother's breasts. He's been chasing big ones all his life!'

'Anyway, it doesn't "akse" anywhere on this form here what size bra your mother wears. And I don't like big ones either!'

'Whooy!' Ossi looked up at me. 'Bella have small ones, eh?'

'Yes Ossi. And they don't have milk! Look some in the fridge if you want.'

'Whooy!' Stretched himself out on the bench and rubbed his belly.

Cliff pretended to help finish the form. Both of them drank milk with their dinner that night. The wine tasted 'ole-like', they said.

*   *   *

Just so, from one to the other. From man-friend, equal in sex, to boy. Like it doesn't trouble him.

'It doesn't trouble you?' I asked Peter.

Something I notice all the time, big men behaving like boys, young men like children. Women too. Carrying on as girls. But at the same time, that's the attractive thing, the spontaneity, the naturalness. The unsteady, uncontrived mess of a growing society. Born in it and still can't make sense of it. Calm and laid-back on the surface but deep undercurrents stirring. Strong tides running, ways and reason setting their own courses.

'You think he sees me as a "mudda" sometimes, Peter?'

Only brief, quickly. And other things crowd in the way. Eyes can't lie but they can hide. Peter stroked my forehead gently but my worries can't rest just yet. Cliff's eyes slinking away stayed in the corner of my vision, a dead spot. Taunting 'cause you can't see it, worrying 'cause you can't catch it. A dead spot.

*   *   *

Just the two of us having lunch at Immortelle Valley Restaurant again, during the week, when Vaughn came stamping in. Hot and sweaty.

'Mr Jagdeo, how you walking so? You shaking up the whole place!'

He gave me a fake smile, stamped over to our table and dragged a chair out. 'I fed-up. Fed-up, fed-up with this blasted place!'

'All right, all right. Calm down, old boy. What're you having to drink?'

'Don' "ole boy" me, I young still yuh-know. Is dis place making me ole!'

Always agitated, speeding up and down in his jeep with a million and one things to do, setting up his own small hotel and restaurant in Store Bay. Calamity clamoured around him, noisy as his mouth that kept running.

'What you so upset about now?'

'Everything! Everything in this damn place there to frustrate you. If you know the bullshit I have to go through to get a liquor licence! Is five months now I up and down, the restaurant open two months already, and they cutting style to give me a damn licence. Them morons it have working for government in town who can barely read! Sitting on they fat arse all day, playing like it's them calling the shots, looking for blasted baksheesh.'

Both Peter and I looked around. 'Bushes have ears.'

Elva raised her eyebrows on a smooth face. Parrot-fish cool.

'Them li'l arsehole! How I could serve proper food without drinks? When people ask for the wine list you have to be there, "Umm, sorry, um . . ." ' He suck-teeth loud and long. 'They there saying they encouraging tourism and same time they digging out people eye.

I don't know what kind'a business that is! You ever see two different airfares anyplace else? Separate price for foreigners? Want the tourist dollar but they don't want the people. Juking every li'l businessman that trying . . . I ain' paying not a black cent more than the damn licence fee. They have to give me it some time! Li'l arseholes in training under the big chief.'

'Watch your mouth, Vaughn, they'll throw you out! You know how they like Trinis already, you're almost "foreigners"!'

'Foreigners! It's Trinidad and Tobago, not Tobago alone. They can't throw me out! If wasn't for Trinidad dis place would sink! Little piece'a island that don' produce nuthing and playing big with theyself. They know they can't run out no Trinidadians, that's what does vex them more. You see what they doing with the Germans? Running them! Deporting de people after they spend all they last two-cent on a property here. After Tobagonians 'self done sell they li'l piece'a acre for ninety-and-how-much hundred thousand dollars, them same arseholes chasing de people out! Refusing them residency. You can't see is madness? Is like a blight! Everything you try and do . . .'

Salad scattered all over his plate, bits on the tablecloth. He stabbed at it some more, voice toning down to story-telling.

'Look the other day, I hire a waitress. Experienced eh, but the girl face sour-sour. I tell her, "You have to welcome the customer, make them want to come back. This is the Caribbean, they hear about our warm and friendly people, they expect to see smiles. When you greet them, try to smile." She turn to me and say, "But Mr Jagdeo, is seven years I been working in Grande Beach Restaurant, is

seven years now they trying to make me smile and I don'
smile yet yuh-know!" Hello!' Waggled his head at me.
'What you go do?! The disease in she!'

Frustration still can't bury the humour in his voice,
performing for us.

'I search high and low for fresh lettuce, driving all up
behind God back, begging for lettuce. Bush growing in
abundance but nobody planting lettuce, it have to come,
cooking, on the boat from Trinidad. I find the precious
salad and rush straight back with it before it could wilt.
Tell them in the kitchen to keep it fresh, in the fridge,
don' leave it out. Come back later and open the kitchen
door. Uh, the lettuce there on the counter looking at me
so . . .' Shrunk down in his chair, hands framing his face,
fingers stuck out like leaves and eyes bugged out '. . .
quail-up, quail-up!'

Peter killing himself laughing.

Vaughn's face sweating, flecks of grey in his hair but
his Indian features still young. Relaxing now, pretending
to sulk. 'No man, it does really try you. I hear they giving
George and all a hard time too. Some "un-unh" officials
asking him about what kind of permission he have to
build this place, how he should move the building 'cause
it's on "historic artifac's". After the man bring in archaeol-
ogists and uncover the "historic artifac's" that they didn't
even know was there! Move the building! The most
environment-friendsy establishment they ever see. And
same time, all the bigwigs bringing they parties here for
luncheons. Huh. Patience eh?'

'Patience with me bartender, have no fear . . .' I half
sang the piece of calypso for him.

'We living a damn calypso in true!'

Softing Skin

Jumped from sleep to living wake by something standing right over me. De black dallie, right close to the bed, a giggle from the floor and Cliff's head popped up.

'Ahh, 'e make you jump, eh?'

'Cliff!'

Peter hadn't stirred. I relaxed back onto the bed. 'You knew it would jump me! What you doing here anyway?'

Cliff, laughing, put his hand on my chest. My fright changing quick to something else. His eyes moving down my naked skin but his hand stayed resting between my breasts. All the flesh in me wanting to curl and arch. Stiffened instead, stayed flat so, my whole body fitting under his hand. Drops of moist under his fingertips.

Peter turned, threw a leg over me, half woke. 'Cliff? What's that thing doing by the bed?'

"E just guarding you, Peeta. Leh me put him back.' Got up and moved de black dallie, lifting him waist and thigh, back to his spot by the wall. Caught sight of himself in the mirror, bare torso twisting to side view, watching me take it in. 'De physical in shape, eh?' Laughing at himself, sitting on the bed, leaning across my legs. 'Bella, girl!' Stroked up my leg pushing off a piece of sheet. I don't have to answer. He glanced at my eyes waiting for his next movement, pushed Peter's leg off but it came back straight away, his hairy arm reached out too.

'What. Peeta, you ain' sharing?'

'Eh?' I grabbed up the sheet and covered my chest. 'What he has to share?'

'Whoy.' He lay down across the bottom, stroking his own chest, smiling at me. Sweetened his mouth and the urge locked in me, flashed in his eyes a second. 'Yuh too sweet, gyal.'

Peter could hear but he didn't move, faking sleep.

Softing Sunday-afternoon sun shining on wet leaves hanging in the doorway. White room, white rafters and a blue plastic rosary slung on the bedpost. Cliff's fingers slipped back up my leg, reaching almost to my hip, under Peter's leg. I reached down and stroked the top of his hand, brushed the warm inside of Peter's thigh.

'Who's grabbing my balls? Ha!' Peter rolled onto his back, we all three laughing, I turned towards him. Stillness heating the whole room.

Cliff's hand stopped moving then slowly crawled to my stomach and down. My body couldn'a hold all the want I have in me. Bursting out my mouth and tongue, my hands and self. Cliff's languid sensual self fired into strong and urgent need. Pushing, greeding, eaten up by all. Straining, fierce pleasure. Sweating, shining sated sex all over him. And us, lying there, tangled tones in blank sheets. The whites of de black dallie's eyes reflected in the mirror.

Sex Talk

SC coming over for the weekend – Small Clit. A friend since university in Trinidad who shared a taste for stupidness and ruderies, a laugh and ballsy talk. She bounced out of Air Caribbean's arrivals and into the car smackkissing and oh-goshing, ruffling Peter's hair. The taxi men she flounced past watched with bottom lips hanging.

'How youall going? Look at you! . . . I all right. Glad to get out'a flickin Port'a Spain though. Oh gosh. I been working hard man, oh jeez!'

'You mean you haven't been getting it?' Peter laughing his big gluga-pipe laugh all the time, all of us making ourselves comfortable in the rude talk. 'What happened to "he of the large dimensions"?'

'He, oh gosh man, dat done. Yuh know how long now dis little t'ing here closed-up. It don' even know how to wink no more, ha!'

'You sounding hard-up girl. Just-now you'll start dribbling like them Tobago men.'

'Oh gosh, no man, they *houngry*.'

The way they watched her was real hungry-looking in true. This is Black Entertainment Princess come true. Visions of African Coca-Cola-bottle figures revolved in their eyeballs, curves with ball bearings for joints, firm flesh bouncing. Tall, neck long and straight, they didn't even have to see her face before the close-up of chocolatey-smooth full features smooched onto their screens. Eye-shadow-dark eyes flicking, mascara lashes on matt brown skin, glistening maroon lips parting. Till she cut the Toni Braxton video playing in their heads with a ice-water look and a long steups. They could smell Trinidad on her after that. Not American but foreign still. Air-conditioned skin, city-style clothes and the confidence in the way she used a car, all set her apart from local beauties. Fellas who ventured a 'pssst' or pitched a kiss while holding their crotch, didn't get a glance from her.

'Oh jeez! What it is wrong wit' dese men! Niggars again, nuh. You could always know them – overbearing.'

Home out of the heat, she started heading for the shower. 'So youall heard from yuh friend Antonio? I ain' seen him in ages.'

Told her yes, he's coming soon to stay with Oliver while we're away.

'He so sweet, eh.' Sailed off down the corridor to the bath. 'Oh gosh! Dat t'ing make me jump!' Landed back in the kitchen with just toothbrush and panties. '*Little Black Boy*! I ain' lying eh, dat is one beautiful piece'a carving youall have in your room there. No joke eh, out of all them things I see dat white woman make, dat is the best. Real real beautiful.'

Told her about Cliff, how in the shower he looked exactly like the sculpture. Even more beautiful.

'Wait nuh. Here? In dat shower? Bella, how youall know this young man? You not frightened?' She stopped waving the toothbrush around and juked out her jaw at us.

'Frightened of what? He's not a criminal.'

The shadow of a cloud disappearing on the sea – Cliff's flash of a mask. Wasn't a crime.

'I don' know. But how youall could just bring him in the house just so? Where he from? . . . Oh gosh, Plymouth. What he look like? Black Chinee? Like the carving but . . .' Reeled her toothbrush forward.

I tried to describe how he dresses, the style of hundreds of fellas in Trinidad too.

'Oh God, one'a them rank li'l fellas!'

'Hear you! He doesn't stink.'

'No, I don' mean stink nuh. Rank, in the way they get on. You sure he not like that? Hunh. I don' trust dem yuh-know. I ain' lying and I know it sound prejudice eh, but if I walking at night and I see a fella like that with he hat turn back to front and a trackpants and a gold chain . . .'

'No gold chain.'

'. . . sorry, but my blood'll run cold. I frighten'a dem. And he black-black eh?' Shaking her head, wagging the toothbrush at me, big brown nipples shaking east-west.

'That'd make your nipples perk up!' Peter jumped in.

She laughed and boxed him, went back down the corridor.

But she would never be walking on a street at night in Port of Spain. And if a fella came walking through her suburbs, he would be a suspect because everyone drove in and out. Safe in her car, if a fella like that was standing by the traffic lights late at night, she'd go through the red light like everyone else, you don't stop. Clothes, cars and subtle shades of skin separate the classes there. The Black middle class distinguish themselves from the working class by dressing the same as their Indian, White, Chinese and Syrian equivalents. The safe middle-class uniform. Men with office jobs, teachers, civil servants, trotting around in little pointy shoes with thin nylon socks. Gabardine pants, pleated in front, with a fancy belt buckle of course. The universal polycotton shirt, shirt-jack, some a tie. Nothing too conspicuous. A gold watch, discreet wristband, gold chain tucked inside the shirt – never too big. Younger men with a tiny earring maybe. Rebellious remnants of ponytails tag a few. The cooler ones challenging with cotton pants instead of gabardine, khaki, polo shirts, Docksiders or even a sneaker-like shoe. Same as everywhere else in the world. The women wannabe'd too, like in the Mutual Life Insurance ad. Nothing too wild or short. Straightened hair, straight skirts and pumps. *Young and Restless* blouses and hairstyles.

None of the big-up fashion of the working class for them. No oversized jeans hanging off the bumsey, see-me-first sneakers, Nike-blazoned tops, huge gold chains and dancehall-queen style women. Fêtes with a whole set of people like that are considered rough by the Trinidadian middle class. They'll have the bad-boy music but not the bad-boy styling. So any fête in Tobago is rough to them because every crowd, even at the Heritage Festival, looks like a Nike fair. The national dress of Tobago for old and young alike, rich and poor – Fila, Hilfiger, Adidas and now FUBU. But it's only the music that's rough here and it's the same rangatang, bad-boy, gagsta-cussin' rhythm as everywhere. Hard-ramming, crowd-chanting, sex-whipping abuse.

* * *

Small Clit lowered her bumsey gently into the lukewarm rock pool. Leaned back cautiously onto her folded towel. Aahing. 'Dis is luvely, eh?'

The three of us in the shallow pool out on the point of Back Bay. Sun slanting straight through the wave crests rolling past our rocks. Perky giant sea horses riding past, necks arched, clear-water manes flicking back. Plunging into brilliant white, churning, frothing. Racing to meet the sun and slick sand. I stretched my legs out flat. Only a few inches of water, warm as my skin. Peter sat with his feet in and we all just watched for a while. Piling rocks nestling close, sharp and crusty, holes and bumps all through them. Jaggedy stiff sponge soaking up the sea's honey. Full of thick starfish-coloured syrup. All the sweetness of the sea. If they weren't so sharp you could just put your mouth and suck it out. Fish, crabs and sea things could come and suck in a bellyful. Ease them from all the salt. But they're devious and sharp, those rocks, slice lines in your hands if you drag on them, gouge out your knees if you fall on them, holding the honey tight inside. The only time they look giving is like now, when the low sun gentles-up on them, rosying the rocks to glowing amber. Then it looks like some drops might ooze out.

A soft wind skimmed a few bubbles on the surface of our pool. Spun them round Peter's feet to the shadowy corner. Left the surface smooth, warm and still. I slipped lower to lie in it. Not deep enough to float me, just the bumps of me, little honey-coated breast islands. A flashy proud sea horse sailed past at eye level, mother-of-pearl and blues glittering and trailing, its sea-eye watching. Another and then another king sea horse. Made you feel rich to see such glory. And hold it for a minute. Just right.

Peter crimped himself in, trying to lie down but he couldn't fit. Rested his head on SC's waist, she shifted it down to her twinkie. He rocked his head comfortably in the dip against her thigh, raised his knees over mine and let his arms float.

'This is so luvely, eh? This spot. Oh gosh man, you could never get this in Trinidad. Two half-naked women? All now so, fellas would be everywhere in them bushes, looking to come and rape yuh tail. Oh shit man!'

Half-laughs rippled the honey. Shifted my waist and a pouf of soft sand mushroomed up.

'Look at you, eh!' SC tweaked Peter's nipple.

'Me?'

'Yes, yuh-know how many a man would give they gold-teeth to be in this position here now?'

'You don't like men with gold teeth!'

'You lucky yuh-know. You lucky to have a girl like Bella too. Yuh wretch you.' Tugged his other nipple hard.

'Ouch! You see how I get molested?' Talking with his eyes closed, waggling his toes. 'And that's not all I have to put up with!'

'Yes, yes! Tell me 'bout dis business with the fella nuh. You have to watch her yuh-know Peter, she like t'ing too bad. You!' She juked my foot, stirring up another cloud. 'How come youall reach so far, man? Three people in bed, oh gosh. That's *ménage-à-twa* man! Jeez!'

'It's not that. There's no love affair going on. But anyway, you wouldn't like that? I mean, two men at the same time. Plenty women fantasize 'bout it. You the one always talking 'bout new things in sex, carrying on 'bout long leather boots and girdles and all kind'a stupidness!'

In broad daylight, talking her fantasies loud and laughing. In girl-talk, telling me details of her let-downs, 'The man keeping on he underpants to sleep!' or delightful surprises, 'Fat like your wrist girl, oh!'

'Two men at the same time? Two totees, one in each

hand?' She materialized a fat one in each hand, looking from one to the other questioningly. Wanked them a little, eh-hehing down in her throat, shaking her tits. 'Eh-hem. Humn. I don' know nuh. I think I would be frightened.'

'You!' Peter chirped up.

'Not by the t'ings nuh. But it's what's attached to them. Dat, I wouldn't be comfortable with.'

'Two men?'

Another peeping sea horse rode by, smiling.

'Anything with a cock. You see two women and a man, dat's fine, I wouldn't have a problem with dat.'

'Well you know I'm here!'

'Shut up nuh . . . but if it's to be three together, I prefer another woman. Anyway, yuh-know me and black man.'

'What about black men?' Peter had joined in late in our friendship. 'I don't see anything wrong with Cliff.'

'He young yet. And he might be different. But most a'them, once you see it comes to they parts, is like they brains down there man.' Talking in earnest too. Always frankly funny. 'They have nice bodies eh, but I don' find them attractive no more . . .'

'Yeah, yeah, I know the rest . . . any halfway decent man is married or gay, then is only the big-belly leftover men. Stella lost her groove story, can't get it back.'

'But is true. Maybe dis fella is different. I hope so. Stella who?'

The shadow of the rocks getting bigger now as the sun set in.

'You sure he not after something?'

Shadows stretched and met.

'No Smallie. He's been in and out our house for two months now and nothing has disappeared. And you know how we live – everything open.'

But his grace had disappeared sometimes. Blanking a worry I couldn't reach. Rough edges peeped out, a glimpse of attitude.

Our skin deepened to red-clay colour and the parading sea horses looked straight ahead now, faces orange. Something sad in the way they dissolved into froth. Something gone, like the heat from the light.

'It's a horrible thing to have to doubt a human being.'

'Mmn.' Peter agreed. 'But sometimes you have to.'

'He sounds different though, dis Cliff. How come he don' mind sharing?'

'Ha! He don't seem to mind at all. He says it's nothing new to him – and he's been having sex since he was ten!'

'I tell you they does get rank. He bold-face eh! How come he ain't frighten'a Peter?'

'What you mean!'

'No, I mean I thought dese macho fellas wouldn't want another man naked near dem for a mile – much less a older white man. You know how they think all white man like the funny business!'

'Who me?' Peter kicking up, flapping as she clapped a hand over his mouth.

'You know what I mean, Bella. He wasn't frightened or tense-up, aggressive? You wasn't scared?'

'Scared?' Scared? All kind of things had gone round in my head but not scared. 'Still can't understand it myself, Smallie. It couldn't have happened if he had hang-ups like that. I don't know. This is the first time this has happened to me.'

We both looked at Peter beating up, and she uncovered his mouth.

'Don't look at me like I'm the expert!' Spluttering, sitting up laughing. 'What – you think I've done this before? Well I never! I was quite decent before I met this wild woman.'

'Hah!'

'Sweetness and light, me!'

'Yeah, yeah.' Splashed him. Wrestled him back down into her lap, Peter surrendering happily, feet up in the air.

'Yes, cool him down Smallie. It's the climate you know. The tropical heat addles the English brain.'

'But you,' she grabbed Peter by the nipple again, 'you don' feel jealous'a this young thing?'

'Oh no.' We watched Peter staring straight up at the clear high sky. 'Why should I?'

'You must! Bella, look Peter getting macho! Playing as if he can't feel nuthing. You really been here too long boy. Bella might get carried away, yuh-know her.' She jiggled his head. 'He have a nice-shaped one? Like yours?'

'You cheeky thing! I know My Dou loves me, that's not the worry. It tests all kinds of limits in a very erotic way.'

'Wha'a . . . Bella, you hear dat?' She leaned forward and peeped in his eyes. 'The man in luuv. And sexy too! Oh gosh.'

Peter blushed and pushed his chin up to the sky.

'Allyou real lucky to find each other yuh-know. Real lucky, eh man. Gi' me a piece a white meat any day. But I glad for you girl. You deserve it after them nightmare years you pass through.'

Sister-sister talk now. On campus we had our nights pushing ourselves down in pitiful talk, then raising-up, strong long-suffering heroines. After, we could laugh 'bout it. When I started living with Peter, the strain of a straight-looking white man came between us, till she found us naked one day, Peter not bothering to cover up, just put back his head and continued sunbathing. SC looking straight there. 'Oh shit man! Oh gosh, you didn't tell me Bella! Or else I would'a introduce myself like this . . .' She bent over from the waist shaking an imaginary hand above her head, 'Nice to meet you!' face pushed out, gawking at some balls.

'Hah! Youall wicked though. And Peter look so decent! I know you wild-up, but look at him!'

Lips turning out, smiling, she looked out past Peter, to the metallic horizon, thinking about some wickedness, shaking her head. Peter's gluga-pipe slid quickly up and down his neck in a silent chuckle.

Our honey pool half in shadow now. Cooler, thinner liquid. Blood gone from our fingertips leaving them wrinkled. Black holes in the rocks bigger, all the warmth in the sun gone. Soon the sun itself would go and leave us. Leave us with a night breeze coming round the rocks licking at wet skin, pinching our nipples. Leave the sky with a taste of light, shadows swallowing up the rocks till they're jagged black, locking away the sea's sweetness tight in their depths. The sea horses would stop shining, fade out to grey then white, rolling rhythms in the night, waiting for moonlight to dance. We roused, pulling each other up and wrapped quick in towels.

'Wicked people.' SC still thinking 'bout different positions. 'Wicked.'

'Wicked my arse!' I laughed back.

'Is full of sand!'

Shadow Mind

We spent that night eating, laughing, relaxing in our friendship. Monday morning we were all travelling, SC back to Trinidad, us to Dominica to see my family. Dropped off SC at the airport first thing. Straight dress and hair set, she was already into hustle-bustle work, don't-give-me-no-chat mode. Rushed back home to finish packing and get ready. Peter came out of the study with my handbag.

'Where'd you put the cash we had?'

In my purse on the couch with my bag. In the study there. No, I wasn't sure, maybe I left it in the drawer. But we searched everywhere and couldn't find it. The study door wasn't locked that night but it couldn't be a thief – Smallie was sleeping just next door with her bag and money right there.

Hustling to catch our flight, Thomas trying to help. 'You sure you brought it back from the bank?'

Yes, I was sure. 'We'll have to get some more at the airport or when we get there. It must be somewhere in the study. Thomas, could you give the study a thorough cleaning and check for it?'

A thousand dollars! I can't forget where I put a thousand dollars just like that.

'Check the bookshelf.' Shouted out to him from the car window, making sure Oliver had packed all his things, shoes, Peter had the passports and tickets, putting on my watch and strapping up my sandals, trying to daub some lipstick on.

All through the flight I rummaged in my head looking for the money. Repeating myself to Peter and tracing back. The feeling that I had left it in the purse was strong but not complete.

'Maybe it's SC,' Peter half suggested.

'What!'

Must be a joke. But that was all he could come up with . . . if I was sure I left it in my purse.

'You never know. Some people have behaviour they can't control.'

But Small Clit a klepto?

'If it's in the house it'll turn up, stop worrying now.'

Next day Thomas called. Hadn't found anything in the study and he'd vacuumed every spot.

'I'll go on checking round the house though.'

But I'll search for the cash myself when we get back home, retrace steps, call SC. Maybe it was when we stopped at the supermarket – stolen from the car then. No use in going to the police anyway.

We were supposed to be in Dominica until the following Sunday but after three days Peter got a call to be in Port of Spain for an urgent meeting. Oliver hoorayed it, eager to get back to Tobago, to his best friend. I called Thomas to tell him we would get in that evening. He still hadn't found the cash, voice softening as if breaking the news of a death.

'Ah search high and low eh Bella, nuthing. And Cliff called for allyou. He say he have some trouble wit' de police. I ain' quite understand too well, but something with some t-shirt he have and de police try to say he t'ief it. He want yuh help. I tell him allyou wasn't coming in till Sunday, anyway.'

Cliff. Police. No, it can't be him. Guilt brushed my conscience for even thinking it and I tried to push it from my mind.

We got home on the last flight from Trinidad, the pizza run. Not a Pizza Hut in Tobago, so the farewell fast-food smells of Piarco Airport followed us into the small plane. Warm greasy cardboard steam rose from people's laps filling the cabin before take-off, competing with the body-odour seats and the finga-lickin' fumes of KFC being eaten in row five. Was always a pleasure to get into one of the big old American taxis in Tobago and feel the clean night air come streaming in. The taxi man quiet and the road empty and smooth. Peaceful darkness expanding all yourself. It always relaxed your travel muscles and by the time you neared home, it'd soften your eyes so you could see all the dim details.

Tucked in Oliver. Turned off all the lights in the house to soak in the back-home-again warming. Even on a black-moon night the beauty in this house could make you weak. A strong black-and-white photograph. Grainy wall faces, clean tile lines, leaf patterns trapped, dappling. Sharp angles of steel overhead, anchored. Fretwork shadows gracing the corners of the corridor with moth-wings, two mongoose heads meeting over the kitchen. And then the sea. Tonight a hollow echo, an inky surface blotting into the night sky. Relaxed on the settees. Still. Bamboo fanned its feathery pattern across the canvas above.

Suddenly, the stiff ficus branches screeched against the wall, a soft smack of bare feet and a shadow scatting onto the terrace. Pelted me straight over to Peter's settee, he shooting up straight.

'Oh shit!'

Cliff's voice.

The figure slouched. He crumpled and sank down onto the bench out there. My heart budduping like twenty horses.

'Oh shit? Cliff? What the hell you doing?'

'I sorry! Sorry. Oh shit.'

Peter leaned back. Cliff nursing his head.

'Come here.' Pieces of my insides still beating-up, a part trying to play cool like Peter but something else leaking under my skin. He came and sat on the edge of my settee and I went back to my spot.

'What the hell you think you doing?'

Breathing hard as me, his answer coming slow. Thought he would surprise us. He didn't have any shoes on. Didn't we lock the gate? I didn't hear any gravel, no dog . . . and why did *he* jump? And run *away* from us?

'So why you run? You jumped further than me. You scared me!'

'I jump when I see allyou, I ain' lie! I didn' expec' you to be sitting here with the lights turn-off. I jump, no joke. All me blood beating. True, feel me heart.'

My blood beating too and my brain fast, batting all over the place. Cliff flopped back, wiped his hands over his face and let them drop. Peter still cooling, silent. Sneaker fumes rising from Cliff's feet, stale sweat mixed with fresh spread from him in the stillness. He tucked his feet and sat up as if to hold it in. Just stayed tight-up. I went for some water.

Turned on some lights. His shoes were near the door by the bedroom, not by the front door. The lights showed up what he was trying to hide: hair fuzzy from neglect and a smear of shame on his face. He suddenly looked years older. A glimpse of what he would look like in his thirties.

I stopped by Peter's side. 'When did you come in? How come we didn't hear you? We weren't supposed to be back here, you know.'

'I know, I know, T'omas tell me allyou was coming in Sunday. But I see allyou pass in a taxi, so I say let me come and surprise you. If you was sleeping, I didn' want to disturb nobody.'

So why his shoes by our bedroom? The door was open, bed visible, us not in it. Whites flashed at me, caught my eye. But I hadn't said anything. Peter did, asking what was all of this about some trouble with the police.

'Yeah boy. If I tell you t'ings dat happen since allyou go away, eh. First time I ever reach in de lock-up. Peeta, if you hear what happen eh. Yeah boy.'

We didn't realize he had reached as far as the lock-up, the police station.

'Dem police hold me fuh a t-shirt I was wearing. Dey say I t'ief it, but is buy, I buy it. Dey hold me in de lock-up in Scarbro police station and then dey bring me in de courthouse.'

Raised up a haggard face to Peter. Peter still didn't say nothing.

'When this happened?'

'Sunday night dey hold me.'

Some relief slowly circulated. The money had gone while the police had him. All shades of doubt eager to run away.

'So, they charged you for what exactly?'

'Somet'ing dey say 'bout "stolen goods". But I tell dem I buy it.'

'It could still be stolen goods. They should be going

after the person selling them. Where'd you buy this t-shirt?' Peter still looking up at the canvas, Cliff leaning forward to him.

'A man. I buy it from a man. He was selling t-shirt and t'ing. I ain' akse him where he get it. I ain' know is t'ief, he t'ief it.'

'You know this man? He's from Plymouth?'

'No. But I see he a'ready. I believe he from Mount Pleasant.'

'And you didn't tell the police that?'

'Yeah, but dem ain' take me on. I didn't eat nuthing from Sunday night till Tuesday. Nuthing. Two night I spend in dere and I never want to reach back in dere nuh. Stink! De place stink'a shit and blood. Turn me stomach. And right where they throw you, is right there you have to sleep, there on de ground. Cockroach walking on you.' Looked at me. 'Bella, all me skin still crawling. I get magger-magger and I feeling ole. I ain' go home yet, I went by a friend in town.'

'Your mother doesn't know?'

'Yeah, she bring food fuh me in dere, but I couldn'a eat.'

'Well, what happened in court?'

'Dey tell me I have to come back next week.'

'How come they could keep him in the police cell for such a small thing?' I turned to Peter.

He explained that when they arrest you, they can detain you for up to forty-eight hours but then they must take you before a magistrate and it's for the court to decide if they can keep you any longer. But the court doesn't have to deal with the case then. It will just set a date for you to appear.

'You really look meagre,' I told him. So different in

just a few days. Who I'd touched and stroked, kissed – a stranger. Thrown on a stinking concrete floor.

'Yeah boy, all me ribs showing.' He lifted his shirt and checked his abs.

'You want something to eat?'

'Na, no t'anks. I ain' feeling to eat, dis t'ing have me whole self turn-round. Sunday I was feeling good-good, and now I feeling beat-up and tired, boy. All me head hurting. I can't sleep, I only studying how dis t'ing happen to me, boy.' His hands harassed his face again, eyes flashing at me between his fingers. Cracked his knuckles, shifting in himself.

'Well it's no good worrying about it. You'll say you didn't know it was stolen. They'll still convict you but it won't be a major fine. But they didn't have to lock you up at all. They have all the evidence they need with the owner, they could have just told you to turn up at court.'

'Yeah, dey advantage me, en't Peeta? But I ain' going inside'a dere again. I frighten! Dat is like hell in dere. And you can't do nuthing fuh yuhself.'

I went to get him something to eat anyway. Thumbed him to the table to eat.

'Na boy. I never want to see inside dere again nuh.' He tried a small forkful, smelling it before putting it in his mouth. I brought him a glass of milk.

The slouch on him, the stink and weariness, were the marks of police hands. They'd be looking to pick on him again. Or it was their warning. Scarring him with adulthood. Overnight, from a youth to a hard-face man, his beauty sunk down inside him.

'Eat something, take a hot shower and get some sleep. I'll put a towel and some clothes on the spare bed for you.'

Peter and I went to bed but my brain still racing fast. Cliff's shoes still in the corridor outside our bedroom, haunting me.

Kitchen Talk

Next morning, after breakfast in the kitchen, I told Cliff gently he should go home, let his mother and Ossi know he's all right. Peter told him never, ever to come creeping into the house the way he did last night. Told him so strong, it was embarrassing. Thomas's eyes met mine quickly and looked down. Cliff still looked shaken up, even more strange in a plain t-shirt and Peter's shorts, Thomas trying not to look at him as he put on his shoes and left. My feelings as mixed up and odd as the changes on his face.

Thomas's embarrassment at a young man who had nothing to do with his days, stayed with us after Cliff had left. Like he had almost expected something like this to happen but wasn't going to say.

'If you know what really happened with Cliff,' I told him. 'The trouble with the police was because he bought a stolen t-shirt. It sounds like they have it in for him.'

Thomas looked down at his broad feet and then out the kitchen doorway.

'Eh-heh? I had a mind was somet'ing worse than dat happen. Dat was Sunday night right? Oh, okay. 'Cause yuh know what I was t'inking!'

Laughing now, our doubts and worries clear enough. Thomas's embarrassment – suspicion – from the first day Cliff had come.

'Dat was the first 'ting dat run through my mind, "I

wonder if dis boy . . ." but then I say look, let me not put doubts in allyou minds. And then again, look how long he been coming round here. If he was like that, t'ings would'a done gone missing a'ready. Is a temptation yuh know Bella. I respec' the way you trust people. I admire dat but I can't live so. Don' mind me talking out'a turn but people have to have they place. You never know how some can take it. Yuh never know.'

But I knew what Thomas thought of anybody who couldn't read, who couldn't speak properly or dress properly. Worse, them who didn't even try. Those who wear their ignorance and background like a style – criminals. I didn't know if he could've seen any evidence against Cliff though. Style can't make you suspect. Not wanting to work – having nothing to do with his days – dirtied his skin, stuck like a piece of snot on his face but it can't make him a suspect.

'There's no way he could've done it Thomas. He was in the lock-up on Sunday night. That money must have been stolen from my handbag in the supermarket car park before we got home that day.'

He wrung his mouth down, shrugging, 'I s'pose so. In a way I glad he was in de lock-up.'

Couldn't tell if Thomas was really as relieved as me.

The fiddlewood trees just outside the door laden with white blossoms, buzzies hustling round, busy needling themselves in. Way down below, Sugar Rat picked his way across the rocks, out to search for conch. We moved closer to the door.

'But dese police'll always be after dese young fellas yuh-know. What you expec'? Specially as he not working. Because is true – where he getting money to buy t-shirt from?'

'Mudda.' I guessed. Wasn't unusual or extraordinary. It's what's the norm for the average young man that's the mystery.

Thomas knew well. 'But that is the next t'ing. He don' be shame to akse he mudda for money, big man like he? I would be shame! In Scarbro too, men does be sponging women while they liming all day round dem rumshops.'

'A lot'a them fellas in town taking more than rum, Thomas. Half'a them look stoned, you can see they red-red eyes. And some definitely on crack. If you know the symptoms, you could spot them.'

'Well is dem I frighten. I know them ones smoking they ganja ain' so bad but is de wild-eye ones round by the market place. They rough. You could see natural that they rough. Like they could do you anything. At least is not as bad as Trinidad though. It have places there you can't pass at all.'

'I know. Look, yesterday's *Guardian* have a church minister saying even his ten-year-old knows where the crack houses are, where the stuff's sold. Me asking how come the police don't know? Ridiculous for them to pretend so.'

'Na man. Dey getting dey little pay-off. Ain' no way that could be going on right dere and they ain' getting something. Dey getting dey little t'ing regular.'

'But no, it's not half so bad here. It changing quick though. You never used to see burglar-proofing in Tobago. Now, look how many houses have it. You notice all them ads for security companies appearing? And all these politicians can say is that is Trinidad's fault. "Rotten eggs coming over here and spoiling the place". But the rotten eggs done hatch local chickens! Just up the road in Prospect village you can buy crack.'

Thomas wiped the sink and flopped the dishcloth. 'I

don' know eh, Bella, you t'ink Cliff on drugs? Although he ain' t'ief nuthing but . . . he look so mash-up just-now.'

How could he be on drugs? Never noticed any signs of it. True he was mash-up last night but that's something else. According to Ossi he has a bad chest and gets sick if he smokes. I didn't know no more than Thomas. Didn't dare to wonder.

Cyarlton Gyardner arrived at the front gate.

'M'arning, m'arning!' Lifting down a cardboard box from his head, not bothering to wipe the sweat beading and running all down his face. 'M'arning. How you doing today? Yuh still don' need a gyardner? Heh, heh!'

'But Carlton, you know you don't have no time!'

'Heh! Yeah, 'cause is three people yard I minding and then I have me own gyarden.' Googly eyes rolling behind thick smeary spectacles, lips skinning back laughing and always talking loud. Must be hard of hearing as well as short-sighted.

'But I go get me . . .'

'Yes, yes, your cousin. But I seen your cousin already – he's the cutlass gyardna!'

'No, no. He could work yuh-know. I could supavise he.'

I watched him in one googly eye and he skinned-teeth wide again.

'A'right, a'right. I have some nice zaboca and coconut dis morning, ah know you does always take some coconut water. It ain' have much else bearing right now. Might get some pommecyterre next week, yuh want?'

The box was full of huge warm avocados, shiny green.

'They good? Ready to ripe?'

'Yeah yeah, they lovely zaboca, man. They will ripe by weekend.'

Back in Plymuth

Plymuth quiet this morning. Tomo and he fellas nowhere around. Masta Barbar alone in he shop, cleaning he blades. Call out 'Cliff'. I don't answer. A couple'a Ossi li'l friends outside Arnold Minimart. They look like li'l boys too, face plain stupid-looking, watching me. Ain' know if to smile or straighten they mouth, eyes don't know where to rest, nor they hand or they foot. Standpipe on the corner left open, water busy gushing out, loud glitter in blazing sun. I turn up into we gap and Lynette spot me from the front porch. Old coral pathway going up to the steps, clean, she sweep out all the leaves round the house a'ready. I don't tell her nuthing. Pass round the back and through the kitchen door.

'Whe' Ossi?' I call out to her.

'Wha'?' he answer from the bedroom.

Ossi lazy self just wake up, face still swell-up, bed-sheet marks on he skin, sitting in the back doorway, one foot bracing, the other splay outside. He watch me from me foot go up.

'Wha'?'

Peeta clothes on me make me feel stranger in the poky room. Scrappy old room. Is what the police do to me – make me stranger to meself. Advantage me. I pull off the shirt and set down on the bed. Ossi still watching me close, like he looking for some reason. Rest me back on the bed. Bare galvanise over me, crosswood with nails juking through. One or two'a the nail ends knocked to lie down, some barely reach through the wood. Old bills stuffed between the rimples'a the galvanise, there still, drying up brown. The paper must be cripsy.

Day now making hot and I feel it pressing through the zinc sheets. Pang . . . crack . . . hotting-up sounds aksing 'wha'?' Walk through the valley, I fear no pestilence . . . Fire-breath scorch down from the roof but a breeze come through and lick me body cool. God is my witness and 'im ah me evidence . . . Lynette broom scratching the front porch. This place tired'a living. Ossi must'e looking out the window 'bove me head, watching them few young pommecyterres swinging on the tree. Or he just looking at the wall at the back, mouth open, thinking he own business. Baby Keisha quiet. *Strangest feeling I'm feeling. Oh Jah love I will always believe in. Though you may think I wait in vain* . . . Only the ticking, cracking roof and a heat in me head.

Court First Time

They had bring me mash-up how I was, from the police station to the court. Take me from the van to go downstairs in a next lock-up. Other fellas in there waiting. Police not saying nuthing, blam the iron gate and lock it. A steps going up and crowdie sounds coming from up there. 'All stand!' a police bawl and upstairs get quiet. Then a police signal a next one, signal the one with the keys and he open the lock-up and point up. Send all six a'we up the steps, lime-green concrete walls, rubbed nasty going up, like where dogs keep wiping theyself on a wall. They put we to line up in front a bench. People full-up the big room, police uniforms everywhere and the judge high-up in a box. Big men in jacket and spectacle, big books, a lady with plenty paper on she desk. And everybody watching straight at we. The room only getting big-up, louder in me head, me eye looking for a place to rest . . . me hand. Look where I reach now. Set down and I so glad we not facing them pack-up bench, we not even facing the boss man in he box. Teeny gold specs slide down he nose, broad forehead, shave-clean, couple grey hair speckle he head. Face open, could'a only be a judge, teacha, docta, something like he is.

Them misters in jacket boxing they books, writing and one talking important, clattering-up me head and this place . . . bail for somebody. One'a the fellas next to me watching a jacket mister strong, waiting to ketch some words he know. The mister going on with 'discretion' and 'client', words so soft you can't hear. The fella next to me straining, lean forward on he knee, a vein by he forehead beating. The smell'a the police on me. Frighten block-up in me. 'Level of 'zasperation'. Not a soul can understand what going on. People getting restless on the benches, shiffing and whispering. Them beefy police by the door smell out the loud ones and skin-back they eye on them. Heavy, tired-face muddas there, set down square, watching they boys in the box. Me mudda can't even reach here yet. See me here in this court – is not me, eh. One short fella by me, watch he mudda face and it burn him. A raging fire start up in he, trimble he fingers, clamp down he teeth. He alone know what he go do when he loose out.

A police by the judge stand up talking, calling he 'Your Worship'. Your Worship this, Your Worship that. Is charge they go charge me. I ain' bound to make jail. A fella name call and a next police signal he to stand, to take out he hand from he pocket. 'Housebreakin'... something a weapon... a cutlass, resistin' arres'... The same fella with the fire in he. They signal he to stand. 'You want to say anything now or wait until the trial?'

The heat in he swell he mouth and tongue, thicken-up he voice. 'I ain' have nuthing to say.'

'Bail two thousand dollars.'

But that vex the fella more.

A next one stand up. 'Robbery with violence.' Is convic's. All the fellas set down next to me is convic's. And is a t-shirt I here for, a t-shirt. Sweating cold and stink, waiting.

The roof high up holding off the heat stacking outside. Ears still straining. Names pulling people to stand up, frighten, don't know wha' happening, waiting to hear what Our Worship have to say. Police call me name and I stand. Me ears close down and a spin going round in me belly.

'A t-shirt sir. He had it on wearing.'

Going round like a sink'a water, dragging me. Our Worship watch me over he specs, I hold the wall and try to watch him clear back.

'Twenty-third'a March.'

'Eh?'

'Next week, you have to come back next week.'

They shoo me from the box, out through the front. Just so they done with me. All them people watch me mash-up self pass, police turn they scorning snout. One stop me by the door. 'You hear, eh? Next week, Thursday. De twenty-third'a March. Come early!'

Outside I see Mudda reach.

'I was trying to find yuh uncle, de one in de force. What dey tell you?'

She and the uncle is the same kind, couldn'a never be there when you want.

Rain Out'a Season

Now in the middle'a this dry season, the sky set-up. Sea set-up here too, out on Plymuth Point rocks. Rain coming. From all the heat that pass a'ready and scorch the land, rain now looking to come. In the middle'a a dry season. Nuthing have time nor place now, not even God can control he business no more. And the sea like it. Watch it chipping 'eself with the breeze. As the sky damp down and get darker, is so the sea copying, waiting. Rile-up and wicked, more ready for the rain than the sky 'self. I stoop under the rock ledge, out'a the wind and set to watch a senseless thing happen. Rain in the middle'a a dry season. The turnin' trees and yellow hills get ketch by surprise. Stand-up with they eyes wide open and clothes strip off, no shelter to run to. A pirogue butting the waves, hustling to get in, a few birds wild, skittling past, fighting back the wind. Sea turn up 'e colours sharper, deeper and lighter stripes. And then the rain start sweeping. Just a few drops pelting here but a sheet coming steady from a far ways out. Closing down the sea, rushing coming in with a breeze fanning in front, making them trees dig they toes in the ground, bracing, naked and frighten, mouth open to bawl but no sound coming out. Grey rocks in front'a me turn wet black. Sand-rocks soaking in the drops, crabs scampling down into the water. Sea send out some mighty big waves, raise-up and rolling in fast, racing to reach the land and soak it before the rain. But this rain sheeting in, suck out all the strength from the sea, all colour from everything. Lashing coming, overtake them waves and whip the land. Trees taking licks, streaks raining blows on hills disappearing quick, gone. Only white and grey humps left, and the stinging rain voice that drown out even the sea. Just the rocks close-up scrouch down with me. Black shiny ones outside crying. Little rivers waggling away loose bits'a sand. Can hardly see the water toes at the end'a the rocks, peeping out from under the white blanket, floating up and down. And the rain shushing, slicing and shushing with the wind behind it. Chicken flesh grow on me skin, little bumps raise-up. Ice run from me foot right up to me ears. A shiver. In this cold whiteness the sea come like a dead body. Dark, grey and swoll'n, rain pocking holes in 'e skin, floating it and sliding it around. Dead feet bumping the rocks and another sheet'a rain fan past on its way to cover down the hills. A coffin shroud. Chicken skin.

This kind'a deadliness is a strange one. Come to show you how small you is. Or how it can take you, just so. Wiping out near everything you can see, that you know is there, making up things out'a water and air. White and grey feelings come to jumbie you. Shushing, cloaking down you brain till you can't tell what time gone, how long you dead and driffing, floating with glass eyes open and rain beating on them. Me leg ketch cramp, I shift and straighten it out in front'a me.

As it come, so the rain going, lifting off the whiteness as it leaving, ribbons dribbling past. Shreds and shadows left in the creases'a hills, between rocks, still whispering shush. White-rice grains'a rain falling silent and straight down now, see them slowing 'gainst the colours coming back out. Wind gone with the rain. Sea sulksing and li'l dripping trickling sounds waking up round me. One'a the crabs peep over the top of a rock. Suckershells crackling, drinking. Hills showing up theyselves, yellow brighter. The trees with they skin darken wet, trying to lift up they green. But none couldn'a figure the reason why. Where the rain come from now, where it going?

Our Worship Sir

Was in Court Number Two I had to go and waste my time, up in front, close behind a jacket mister who busy-looking, turn-page reading and pulling he fat nose. The room small, like a classroom and the teacher sitting up in the box with a old fan by him. Dwarfie school desk and chairs on one side, scratches all over the benches, corners rubbed down by nervy hands, varnish wear-off the edges. The place smell hot and dusty like a classroom too. Only thing missing is chalk. No use, nuh.

'Gilbert Ramsey! Gilbert Ramsey! No appearance, Your Worship.'

'Pauline George! Pauline George! No appearance, Your Worship.'

'Twenty-ninth'a June.' Teacher look at the lady sitting behind a desk by him.

She look up at him and raise-up her pencil-line eyebrows. 'Yes, I hear you.' She keep them raise-up and write the date, scratching she head with the top'a the pen, fingertips stubby and round-off from housework like Lynette own.

'Terence Samuel! Terence Samuel! Present, Your Worship.'

The fella come and stand next to me, Mr Jacket still reading and writing on some yellow paper.

Teacher flap he hand to the police by him. 'Prosecutor?'

'PROSECUTOR' mark-up on he fat black book so

everybody could know is he own. Voice deep-deep to fit a man looking like he. Short and red, he head like a rock, chin square-off and forehead squash down he nose. Big Pro. He voice come from down by he belt, boom round in he broad chest spanning he uniform button tight.

'. . . Unable to proceed today . . .'

Miss Eyebrow inspec'ing she big grubby book, taking she own sweet time.

'. . . Come back on the twenty-sixth'a June . . .'

The fella go back outside fumesing. They wasting people time.

A rough-up fella on the bench next to me. Scar-up all over he head and neck. Piece'a ears gone, a old tom cat – head and neck in one, shoulders tough and thick. A damage-look in he small eyes, like he brain beat-up too. Take he two big-skin hands and scrub he shave-head and face, set back looking out the louvres.

Outside, the sea chilling, looking close like a wall going up to the sky. Hot sun scorching rooftops in town to a red-tin desert. Bus sounds and music from the market square, stifle and smuthered. Fort Granby outline 'gainst the sky and, lower down, the tall church tower with the balls balance right on the end'a the points. A old lady come out'a she kitchen squinting and go down she back step, one at a time. Heat whiten she hair more and dance like glass off she galvanise roof. Broad bright green banana leaf waggle 'gainst the louvres'a the court, dodging a hot breeze driffing in – the only living colour 'part from the sea. Tom Cat stretch and yawn. Time stretch 'eself too.

Next case is Tom Cat own. When he name call and he stand up, the back'a the class start sniggling and holding in laughs. He pants tight tight and pinch-up in he bumsey.

Crook he knees and pull it out, fix he balls and spin a finger in he nosehole.

Like all'a them know Tom Cat. Big Pro smiling, call the wic'ness – is a old man, all excitey, getting on 'bout what Tom Cat do he, t'ief he food, all kind'a thing and how he go 'chop he up'. Big Pro cool he down, them jokers in the back laughing.

In a silence, when teacher busy writing, Tom Cat let out one loud belch. Miss Eyebrow duck she head giggling and Tom Cat start fanning. Fanning the stink belch slow over to Big Pro. Set them off laughing again. Teacher patience done. Wasting people time. The wic'ness carrying on again. And all when he finish done and they shoo he from the stand, they only give Tom Cat a small charge – a two-fifty – and tell he 'he get off light'. Tom Cat vex 'cause he want a 'lickle two-months' instead, he like it inside the town house. Brace heself back on the bench steupsing and watching the sea.

Mornin' dragging 'eself into the next case.

'Lucille Smith!' A woman get up from a bench behind.

Teacher take off he spectacle, rub he eye and wave she to the stand. She squeeze past, brushing she bumsey on Big Pro desk to step up onto the small box.

'Hold the Bible with yuh right hand.' Miss Eyebrow say from behind she desk.

Pro get up slow, scraping the chair and running he finger inside he belt, clearing he chest. Teacher put back on he spectacle and look out the window. He is a Indian-mix man, must'e from Trinidad. Hair stand up, comb back sharp, make he look stric'er. Serious face, eyes quick, he hand tired'a writing.

'Tell the Magistrate your name and where you live,'

Pro rumble, swelling he chest and rolling he hand towards Teacher.

She start, Teacher writing down, the woman talking and looking up at the ceiling, roll she eye to Pro when she finish.

Pro breathe in deep. Important. 'Do you remember the day of the sixth of October 1998?'

'Sixth'a October?' The woman rolling she head quite back now. Pull-in both'a she lip and bite them, look down, check each side'a she jeans-pants.

Big Pro turn to her.

'I t'ink so, heh.' Shame and smiling, getting on like a li'l girl. She almost big-size like Pro. Hair paste back neat, face shining with Vaseline, t-shirt with a gold print spanning she waist big as she bosom.

'You think so?'

'Oh yeah, yeah I rememba. Un-humn yes.'

'Where were you at six-thirty a.m. that day?'

'Six-t'irty in de evening? I was home.'

'No, A.M. In the morning.'

'Oh A.M., right.' Tap she head, hold on the stand and brace forward. 'Yes, in de morning,' she get it, 'I was home. Dat was when Georgie come and tell me dis fella break-in me shop. Georgie does live by me, he ketch . . .'

'Hold up! Hold up.'

Them police in the back chucking small laugh at the woman stupidness. Big Pro heself smiling at Teacher and swelling up he chest to continue.

'You can only say what you saw, only that.'

She watching the fella next to me and he stare she back, bold-face.

'Where is your shop located? . . . So it's part of a big building . . . And the building is made up of what?'

'Wall. Is a wall building.' She look at Pro like he should know better, he must know the concrete building heself but Pro looking at Miss Eyebrow and they shaking they heads together.

'And the shop is in this building? How many openings?'

'Opening? I didn't leave nuthing open.'

Gaffles from the back.

'No. Doors.' Roll her on with he hand.

'Well, it have a sliding door to the front and two half'a door to the back.'

She feel good with she answer, nod and plunk she hands behind she waist. Look down at Pro sideways. She ready again but 'two half'a door' echoing round the back'a the room. A police hold up three fingers and slapping the bench. Pro smiling round. Teacher have to watch outside for patience.

'So how many doors? Two half'a doors is the top and bottom of one door and the one in front makes two?'

'Yes!' Like this big police couldn't count. 'Two half'a door . . .' she pointing top and bottom '. . . and one in front . . .' thumb she hand over a shoulder, '. . . two door!' She stance waiting, eyes turn up to the ceiling.

'Now, the doors, how do you secure them?'

She wing a look at he and don't answer.

'How do you lock them to secure them?'

'I does just lock them.' She do a key action in front. 'Is a sliding door, I just lock it.' Turn she key again, more firm.

'No, *how* do you lock it?'

She realise he simple now, that's why he smiling so stupid to heself and the fellas in the back laughing at he. Turn square to him, take she hand and draw it out. 'You

156

does have to pull one side across so, to meet the otha
side . . .'

Everybody laughing 'cept Teacher and Mr Jacket.

'. . . And then you does just lock it.' She turn the key
again. So simple. Turn up she hands.

'*What* are you locking it with? A padlock, a chain?'

'A key! You does lock it with a key!' Do it slow so he
can see clearly. Teacher glaring at Big Pro.

'Okay, okay. And the back door, the same?'

'Yeah. A next key.'

'Okay, so the locks are built-in. And what is the front
door made of?'

'Glass. Is a glass door.'

'The whole door?'

'Yes. The whole door is glass. Is a glass door.' Draw a
big box with she two hand.

'Anything else the door is made up of?'

Teacher take off he spectacle and put down he pen.

'Is a sliding door. It make out'a glass. The whole thing
is glass, you could see plain through!' She can't believe
that Pro don't know what a sliding door look like. And
them jokers starting up again in the back.

'But what is *around* the glass!' He smiling again at
Eyebrow. 'The frame, what is the frame made out of?
Wood?'

She give up trying with him, look to Teacher for help.
'How it can make out'a wood? Is a sliding door. I sure
everybody inside'a here know what a sliding door make
out'a. Is not wood.'

Teacher refuse to look in she eye.

'Well, what?'

'A silva t'ing what does be round them kind'a door!'

'A metal?'

157

She fed up. 'Yeah. A silva metal.' Paint it heavy-hand round the door. Done with that.

'Okay, a glass door with a metal frame.' Pro trying to get back serious.

Teacher pick-up he pen but he ain' writing. He looking at Big Pro like he sorry for him. Mr Jacket was listening all the time, acting as if he reading, now he watch Teacher and turn-up he two hand at him. Teacher fedupsie look pass him straight and go back to the sea.

'The back door now. What is that made . . .'

The stupidness I have to stay here and listen at, just to wait for mine to call.

'. . . Do you know Wayne Martin?'

'Look, he right dere.' She fly out a hand at the fella. She waiting again but Teacher take enough.

Mr Jacket stand up. 'Your Worship . . .'

'Yes, I think this is wasting time. The other witness is here?'

'No sir.' Pro mumble, fingering he hat.

'Well, we'll continue this another time . . . and talk to your witness before . . .' Flap he hand from Pro to the lady '. . . try and . . .'

Pro hold he hat and look down like a small boy. Teacher still flapping he hand and fretting. 'Come down from there . . . You can go.'

She still waiting.

'You can go and sit down.' Chase her from the stand and close he eyes, turn to Miss Eyebrow for her to find a date.

Pro and Miss Eyebrow and the rest'a the class shame for the woman, how she can't even answer a few question. But she ain' shame, she don't feel no how. Must be Pro that do something wrong with he big stupid self.

Midday reach. After I setting there all mornin', all they do is to call me name, make me stand up, Pro rumble something and then they tell me I have to come back again. Again. I have to come and waste time. Set down on a hard bench, in a choky room breathing full'a hot people and listen to all'a that. For a stupid t-shirt. I have to come back again.

Nuthing Doing

Heaven don't have no heaven, nuh. I brace-up listening to Tomo and he fellas outside Masta Barbar shop. Shit-talking.

'You didn' see Farma' mudda sheep?'

Dobermann don't know nuthing 'bout that.

'Farma mudda sheep? Wha' happen with it? Wha' I go want t'see Farma mudda sheep for?'

'You ain' hear boy? Farma mudda sheep get brush! Somebody brush de sheep. And kill it.'

'Kill it?'

'Yeah, everybody in Plymuth went and see de sheep. Some fella tie up de two back foot on a branch and de sheep neck chuk between de tree stump. Condoms too, he leave two rubber on de ground right there.'

'He use condom? What de fuck!' Tiny turn round and lash the tree with a stick he have in he hand. 'Condom!'

I know fellas real sick these days. When I see the sheep meself, I say – what really going on in this place? Who the hell know? Not me, nuh. Dobermann cool.

Jukie still want to give he the picture though. 'Yeah boy, 'e force de sheep. Choke it, 'cause nobody didn' hear not a baa. De neck twist and when Farma let down de sheep to the ground – you hear "guuff" – all the wind that was choke-up in it. Stink! Tears come in Farma eye, boy. I feel for he, eh. Was a big mudda sheep. He say, "De po' dumb animal. If 'e could'a talk . . ." Fucking sheep. T'ing like dat never happen in Plymuth.'

'Wha'? You mean, no animal never *dead* from man brushing dem? Rememba Abba and he sheep a'ready? When de sheep bawling 'e say, "Eh, shut-up and take it, yuh sweet maa." Oye! And you don' rememba Ronno and de duck?'

'Plymuth people too nasty.'

'Aye, dat was kicks, boy. Ronno reach in court for dat. Then he turn round and say he guilty, guilty for brushing duck! Aye! The kind'a licks them fellas in de town house give he! Aaye, boy.'

Tiny making a racket, beating up the tree with he stick laughing. Dobermann still cool while them fellas gyaffing and jiffling. This kind'a thing don't happen in he big city ghetto. He check me again. Can't see shit 'pon me face neither. Ice T.

'Ronno get more jail than when Miss Colette son brush he baby niece. Ronno get a two years and Miss Colette son only get a eight months. Brushing duck boy, aye!'

Tiny scratch some sand. Some'a the fellas stop smiling.

'I feel Farma know who do it, though. He say he have a good mind is who. You know Conrad and he brother? One'a them. They had send Conrad to live with he aunt in Lowlands but he had to come back this side – he was causing some interference with dem animals round there. Must watch he, he don' check woman yuh-know. Fucking sheep, huh.'

A couple'a the fellas check each other faces. Tiny watch mine but I hold it smooth and cool just like Dobermann own. Tomo chilling in he vest and slippers, squat down on a drinks crate in the shade.

Lynette passing home from the corner grocery, carrying

Baby Keisha on she side. The fellas watch she swing Keisha down to the ground to walk 'long side her. She broad bumsey cock up in the air for a minute while she tug at Keisha dress. The fellas eyes resting on it. Masta Barbar heself watching. She straighten up, wave at barbar and continue on, bumsey rolling on each slow step, skirt riding up behind she knees.

'Unh.' Tiny look at Masta Barbar, dark in he shop. 'Nuthing doing, boy.'

Nuthing more to do than mind people business. He turn and watch me. Tomo too. They looking to fling talk on me now. The way Tiny mouth itchin', he go start it. All what they want to know, he go broadcast, playing like if he know. Making up things that a piece'a fella like he could'a never get. How the white man need a help-out. How dem women who does be with white man never satisfy. How I does get pay to give she good. How I lucky to ketch a good one so and how she look like she does take it good. He mouth itchin', eye watching me face set. And when he finish telling them fellas, imagining all kind'a ways how I does give she, getting hot heself, jealous'a what he dreaming. Then he go turn it round. Run talk how is not the woman I like – is the man. How she just a cover. Telling the fellas to check de white man and check me. And see if I cutting style on them now.

Destiny, mama look at where you calling. I moving on. Home or somewhere. Where I can't be found.

* * *

Lynette like to watch *Oprey Winfree*. And Ossi does watch it with she sometimes, 'cause he want to see *Young and Restless* and *Bold and Beautiful* after that. Lynette say she is the smartest, most frontin' black woman she ever know. She does give it live and direc' and quick. One'a them people who does be aksing all kind'a questions, wanting to know every damn thing. Lynette don't mind that 'cause she go never ever reach on the woman show and be there talking out she business loud. Could stay here in front the TV giving answer, laughing at people, feeling sorry for them, from right here in she home. Sitting in she brassiere and skirt, foot barely crossing in front'a she, splay-out toes with piece'a green nail-polish left on them.

Oprey big eyes and broad mouth twang out the words just like a honkie, 'Girl, why don' you just git yourself down here?!' Question she face at we and turn clapping somebody on. Lynette 'bout the same size as she and maybe same height. Sitting admiring how the woman hair so straight and skirt-suit fitting so, how she lipstick stay, eye black-liner and skin all-in-one colour. Jealous'a how she can laugh and skin open she mouth, hee-haw joky round the place and still look good. She say how she see Oprey in a flim a'ready and she was plain-looking ugly. Dat's how she does really look when she take off all that make-up and fancy clothes, worse than Lynette. But still, she say, the smartest, most frontin' black woman, and rich too. The girl come on and they smiling, people clapping, they look like two dolly laughing with they white-white teeth out and lip shining. The girl name Halle Berry and Oprey talking sista-talk to she. She talking 'bout being a black actress – that's when we realise she ain' white. You couldn'a tell watching them black women with hair like white people, shaking and all. The girl skin clear, nose small and straight – a talking dolly.

Ads come on. A big black man saying how hard life is sometimes and everybody need a hand so just call 1 800

JESUS. Then one for a 'erbal, all-natural Viagra. That's how them Yankee does talk – 'erbal. They does take the same words and make them nice, Oprey does do it good, she say, 'I use it *like* every*day*!' And 'Girl, you are *wearing* those capris!' *Hot* sound like *hat*. 'So, are you in *luuv*?' The way she say – go *girrl*, *yeah*, *awesome aw*esome, she could get people to do anything. A time she had a white fella who could wine he waist and she make everybody in the place get up and wine. Going *whoo*. She good at that, getting people to go whoo. Lynette say she could stay and listen to Oprey talk whole day. Sometimes Baby Keisha does say half'a word in the TV talk and Lynette does feel real proud, repeat it to the neighbour. When she have a li'l money she does try to buy TV things for Keisha – Ultra Pampers, Pringles, Bounce Fabric Softener even though the clothes drying stiff on the line, no machine to put them in. She must'e dreaming 'bout one.

Foreign is a place that have a thing for everything. Imagine if a body have a garden in foreign, they have to have all these things you see on TV – a lawnmower, a thing for blowing dry leaf, a robowacker – not for cutting bush, they only using it for trimming, trimming lawn edge round a neat-neat house. Then they having three'r four different clipper for neat'ning they bush and cutting they flowers, never use a cutlass. And gloves and a thing spin-ning sprinkling water round and round. Anything you think of, them people in foreign have a thing for it – for cleaning they house window from outside, a hose thing for cleaning they car with soap and water same time. And they must have to have a garage to put all them things in. Two garage even. In they kitchen – if you see things, fit in neat, everything join up in one worktop, stove, sink, the thing they packing wares in to wash, microwave, everything. Clock, radio and always a telephone in the kitchen hang up on the wall. Things you can't even think 'bout, they done have a thing for a'ready – you push a tin can and it cutting open the top one-time, something you put on carpet and it just eat-up the stain like magic.

But the food. Lynette tell Ossi is because in foreign they don't eat real food, that is why they look so, like dolly. Is only clean, wrap-up package food they does eat. Never see them cut up bloody meat or clean a chicken, just take out a thing from the freezer and *pop* it in the microwave and *wallah*. And Big Mac and KFC. All'a that does make them big-up and shine, skin smooth and fair, not a black hole in they teeth. Lynette feel if she really try, if she had money, she could make Baby Keisha look like foreign.

I does watch Lynette. She think I don't know what's in she mind but I know she good. And she don't trust me for that. I know when she watch them people on TV it does burn she. When she see Mr Arnold daughter marry and move out the other day – she jealous. Jealous'a the girl bridesdress, how she marry proper, how she man have a car and the girl gone to live in he parents wall-house. While she, Lynette, on she backside, minding baby without man, scrunting. Making she stingy and restless – wishing for somebody to just take she out'a here.

Always checking on me. She grudge me going by Peeta and Bella, how I could be in they house, in they car. She does akse Ossi things 'bout them – what it is I does be doing there. Everybody only checking my movements, 'cept Mudda. And where she be right now? Who knows what she does be doing when day come. Working how? Pushing what load? She don't care, nuh. Scrunting all she life and still there fighting-up. She with she bossin' self, always bawling, 'Stay out'a trouble, stay home. If yuh don' have no work, yuh have no business outside. And mind the company yuh keep!' She always telling me that and never around to know what it is I doing, who I liming with, only listening to Lynette grumbling. Stay in the house and do wha'? End up like Lynette?

Next was *Bold and Beautiful* again and then *Family Matters*. No action in Plymuth tonight, nuthing going on. Court tomorrow.

Hero Convic'

Just me one on the front bench today. Up and down these people have me for this thing. A wicked-looking convic' fella sitting in the box. Good-looking but like he have something living behind he eyes. Look like he could be one'a them star-boy in a gangsta movie. He know it too. Cool-cool with heself. Even though he come from jail, he looking clean and comfortable. White vest and jeans, a silver earring in each ears, diving watch on he hand, a Reef sandals on he foot, toenails clean. Tall as me and well build-up, he know he good for heself, know what he about. When they call he name, he stand up, foot wide apart, know when to sit back down. And all the time, he eyes eating up everything going on in Court Number One, moving slow, whites clean as he vest. He give me a big-man to small-boy look and done with me. Now he watching the wic'ness coming to the stand. A cat getting ready to jump on a mice. Settle forward onto he knees, neck tensioning, body shifting, eyes scanning the new police prosecutor quick, then fix-back on the mice. The mice is a reddish fella looking like one a'them small thing people does keep for pet. Guinea-pig. The boy have a nose and mouth all-in-one like a guinea-pig. He nervous so, li'l eyes jumpy, noseholes blinking as he go up onto the stand. Hunter Cat smile and settle he haunch down.

The new prosecutor have a posie-face, fat and round all over with a li'l spectacle hook on he nose. Voice raising high and he looking at the rest'a them police when he talking. He nervy just like Guinea-pig.

Guinea-pig turn he nose to Your Worship, blink it and start. People on the back benches listening now, stretch forward to hear better and see the boy face while he telling it.

'. . . In my shop . . . he tell me I have to give him all the money I have behind the counter . . .' Noseholes open and stay so for a while. '. . . Pull a cutlass and hold it against my throat . . .'

A few whispers pass round at that. If was me I would'a give he the money, quick-time too.

'. . . Say he go cut me . . . I was frighten.'

Hunter Cat smile at that, turn he head away lazy when people watch he. Swing back slow to he mice still frighten there, smirksing, waiting to play before killing.

'. . . Take the money and the radio and went.' Leave him breathing hard, chest beating like he nose, he two li'l front paw resting together on the stand.

Posie-face prosecutor look at he police friends and then at Your Worship, meaning I tell you so. Hunter 'lert to the movement and flash he eye to it, then drift back to he corner mice.

'Permission to show Exhibit A, Your Worship.'

Just like TV but you seeing it live and direc'. Po-face take out a wicked-looking cutlass from a plastic bag, hold it up high for everybody to see. The wicked and deadliness'a the pointed cutlass sliver round the courtroom. The lady clerk look at the cutlass then at the wic'ness full'a pity. She take it and show it to Guinea-pig and Your Worship, holding it by the two ends and looking it up and down. Rest it down on she desk and watch Hunter Cat with a turn-down mouth. Hunter Cat just watch she and the cutlass and suck he teeth.

Guinea-pig make he way back down from the stand to go and sit down, weak. Hunter finish with he now, watching Po-face digging in he papers like how a cat does watch a dog, scorn-like. Fed-up watching the stupid dog, he head turn to a woman sitting further down the same bench with Guinea-pig. She youngish, face mannish like he, corn-row plaits going straight back and neck strong as he own. When they eye butt-up he turn away, bite he teeth together and look downstairs to the lock-up like he ready to go, blanking he eye.

Next is 'Constable Detective 745601, present sah!' He come marching in, bow to Our Worship, reach up on the stand and pick up the Bible one-time. Shout out he oath, put hands behind he back and square-up opposite Hunter. Neck choking tight in a collar and tie, uncomfortable in he clothes. Head small and hard-looking and he face ugly. Nose hard-skin and spread-out like it have three nosehole. Pointed bumsey cock-out behind. Iguana he look like – 'guana in shirt and tie. Star-boy convic' can hardly watch he straight without laughing 'bout how ugly and uncomfortable the man is. He check me to see if I laughing too but the lock-up police notice and cut he eye at we.

'... Nineteenth'a March ... O nine hundred hours ... to the home of Laurence Williams in the Signal Hill area ...' Full out he chest, put he hands on the rail and lean forward looking straight at Star-boy '... Laurence Williams in a room, lie down on a mattress on the ground. Sleeping!' Snap it out and jerk he head like he ketch some food.

Star-boy watch him straight and smirk. He remember

that morning too, lean back, cock he head and watch 'Guana from the bottom'a he eye.

'His mother say, "Laurence, look, police come" . . . A warrant for your arrest . . . He didn't say nothing, sir . . . I caution him . . . have to go down to the station . . .'

Star-boy laziness still vexing 'Guana. He working some bumps by the side'a he eyes, neck pump out, set-up to bite. This hero-fella cool as Tupac in a Bronx police station, Yankee cops shouting and spitting in he face for him to talk but he just cool, face smooth, more better-looking than them cops. Rebel leader, drug-war fever, a black boy near to bust. But the fellas in them flims could cuss. Yeah boy, they could real cuss. This hero here ain' saying nuthing. Just taking all people have to say and feeding the thing behind he eye.

'Guana continue with he cautioning. Star-boy ain' taking he on, lean forward and bend down checking he toes.

They push Tupac head down into the police car. The chi'ren in the Bronx come out to watch. Tupac own baby in he child-mother arms watching the cops take him away. He face looking through the back glass, eyes holding onto he baby girl till he can't see she no more.

When Star-boy head raise up, he face wipe clean'a everything. Even he eye don't have nuthing in it. The thing disappear, leave him as if he never do nuthing at all. Watching the woman on the bench like he don't know she, he look at Your Worship, then at the plain wall behind the dress-up 'Guana.

Your Worship read the statement back to 'Guana, rushel the papers and look at some ones he have under-neath. Posie-face waiting, dog watching he master.

'Well, young man. Williams.'

Star-boy already stand up, face still clean.

Your Worship cool as he. 'You see, you're still young, eh? And you been in and out'a there plenty times already. Why, what happen? You know . . .?' He lean back on the cushion chair and beg he hand at Laurence.

Star-boy take a while, check he clean toes again. 'Sir I . . .' Pull up a blank face. '. . . I is a hard-working man.'

'Hard-working man? But when are you getting a chance to work – you always up there! As soon as you come out, you do something again. And violence. A lot of violence. What happen to you, man?'

The thing jump back sudden so inside Laurence eye and he turning round as if he don't want nobody to see. Trying to stop the thing from taking over he whole self.

'I, I have a bad chest, sir.'

The whole courtroom start up. A real Star-boy would'a never say that.

'Is true sir! Akse me mudda! Look, she sitting right dere.'

'A bad chest! A bad chest can make you do all these things? And your mother is here?' Sir look at Laurence with he one hand on he chest, follow he other hand pointing to the woman who look like he. Tupac watch he mama face . . . she nod slight and stare straight back at Your Worship.

Laurence set back down with the thing in he clawing and scratching.

'Awright, awright!' Big Mouth by the door shush people.

'I think we have enough evidence for a case here. A very serious offence. This will have to go for a hearing in the High Court. Do you have anything you wish to say at this point?'

Laurence get up. Everybody waiting.

'Sir.' He voice fighting and he look at sir strong. 'Sir, I don' know nuthing. I have nuthing to say.'

'Twelfth of May.'

Clerk bring the papers for Laurence to sign and he ups and start going down the steps. He is a sorry black man, eh. Tie-up and vex, tired'a shaming heself. Signalling Dear Mama, instruc'ing she to come round and see him downstairs. The lock-up police follow him, unhooking he keys. Laurence never look back once for me, leave me there alone on the bench. Jumping to order like another nenny. Waiting for case to call.

A Suffering Blue

Sometimes the sea is a senseless thing. I does watch it. Going out, coming in, going out and coming back in. That's just the way it is. Is a aimless thing. This morning when I reach right out to the end'a Pigeon Point, out'a the way where nobody does come, tide out. Rocks and sea grass bare out'a the water close to the beach. Hardly a ripple, no colour in the water. One'r two waves driffing in from the reef further out. Shadows dark under patches'a sea grass, bleach out sand pools. No colour, the water have no colour this time on a hot morning. Clear-clear water washing galvanise sand, I can see grains rolling. Is no reason why all the blue have to run so far out. Watch it out there just past the reef, a dark deep line behind white waves. Then from there stretching in, is only flats'a browny-green patches, fading coming in. Maybe the sea just feel to let 'e colour drain out. Like how I does feel on a hot morning like this. No colour.

I take off all me clothes. All. Like how Peeta and Bella does swim. Naked as I born. 'Cause I feel like. Like the sea, coming in, going out for no good reason. Some people does have to have a reason for everyt'ing, else they have to find out why. Bella does be aksing me questions – what I want to do, what work I was doing, if I like it, why I like the sea. I suppose to have answers living in me head all the time? If I like it, I like it. Ain' no good reason I have to know why. That's just the way it is. I see no change. If I want do something, I do it. Yeah boy, just do it. And that's how them flim-star fellas does move. Is only them talk-show people does set down and want to talk 'bout *why* they do this and *why* they do that, telling the whole world they business. It have one TV fella who does make people talk out they whys and what it is they do – till they jump up and fight, grapple and pull out each another hair, fighting like them Plymuth women. On TV and all.

You see me, if I feel to come in, I come in. I feel to go out, I go out. I feel to let all me colour drain out, I just let it go. Far. Deep blue in me head. Cool all the while. King'a the block, man'a the ghetto, I got *juice*. Respect. Respect I man, 'cause I is the real juice, blue juice. Me. Spreading far. Chipping with the breeze, shining-back the sun, doing what the hell I want. Big black waves when I vexing, still clear glass when I chilling. Versatile all the while. I is me own boss.

Sun blazing black on me skin, sitting here. Foot like a piece'a smoothen black-coral resting on the sand. Breeze spinning shallow water past, I push me foot in. Couple lizard fish scatter through the water. Sand diver, Bella does call them. Water show up the li'l cocoa-brown in me skin, lighten it. White heels looking big. Sand soft like wet powder. Close by the sea grass, some egg balls rolling, dark glass marbles. Could watch them all day, how the colours change and shine, purple, green, blue. Bella have all kind'a different name for them same sea things. Algy and annenemy, mussels, mullucks – names she calling from books, names from foreign.

Now I flowing 'cross rocks, from one pool to another, between the coral shelf and beach lip. Flowing currents 'gainst the breeze, tickling sea grass. Two li'l fish showing off they purple and yellow tail, two beads flashing round in a glass bowl in the sun. I ease me hot skin into a deep patch. Deep enough to float me. Swallow me skin like a ice surprise. Dip down me head for the shock to wake-up me scalp and every hair. Bobbling and waving like the shells them crabs carrying, rolling and bubbing. Up top the sky light blue like a mirror on my water. My face is a island. Small waves washing in stronger, pulling reef colours up 'bove the surface. Cool and warm same time, same sea. Tide coming, going out, nowhere else to go. Just a few inches higher or lower. Nuthing doing, just chilling. And all the pose them fellas on the block posing, they ain' doing nuthing either. Them ain' the real thing. Stand up talking shit all day, playing as if they in the middle'a Brooklyn. Never stick-up no grocery, shoot nobody, never even hold a gun in they hand. Nuthing. Even Peeta and Bella in they flim-style house, with they fancy car and foreign talk – they just there, doing what work it is they have to do. And them will always have things to do. Them have it good. On top'a money to spend, places to go, them have one another, family. Easy in life. Ain' even hustling to buy fancy clothes. Bella have a Nike sneaker but she does only wear it when she exercising. When time come to dress up, she putting on a old black shoe to go and dance in Sunday School. They could'a buy any amount'a things they want, latest style and fashion. But them don't like that. Don't want what other people want. They like bush and animal, old boat and old-time house. They like some funny kind'a food and plenty talk, questions. Is so the li'l boy does akse, 'Why?' And Bella 'self – who knows what it is I feel for she? No sense in nuthing. Them good for theyself. Yeah boy.

Me body floating, heels resting on the sand. When

my bumsey bump on the sand I feel it stirring 'gainst my skin. Squingy totee rolling and lolloping like a lump'a sea sponge. Lower down, water shorten me two legs, they snaking. I loose out the pee in me, feel it moving inside me totee, I let it go, warm current on me belly, mix with the cool and warm. Relax in meself. Drift me arms out over me head and me chest raise up. I is a island. Legs open and the floating blanket still holding me. Like a big cape, spreading me far and wide but keeping me safe and gentle. Only heels anchor me down. Only me face showing to the world.

And this world is a suffering blue and blazing sun. Beating on me face. Blue juice floating while me face roasting. I dip it but sun dry it in no time, drink up every drop and start the heat in me head. Heating up me blue juice to red. Dry up every bit'a feeling, every reason to do nuthing. Here, naked as I born, midday shimmying off sand and sparking the water. Blinding me eye. Burning a emptiness in me belly. Boring a silver bullet hole in me chest.

De Car

Thomas performed the story for me at home, excited, panic still rattling him.

'Dat night Bella, I run inside. I say "Antonio! Antonio! De car! De car gone!" Antonio say, "What? Ze car is outside". I tell him, "No, no. De car gone. It not dere!" '

Antonio was staying with Oliver and Thomas while we were away again, in St Lucia this time.

' "T'ief! It get t'ief!" I tell him. "I hear it start up, but I t'ought is you going out. Call de police! I going up de road!" I run down to Prospect. I blowing hard. "Anybody see Mista Johns'n car pass just now?"

' "Yea", they say. "Wha' happen?"

' "It get t'ief!"

' "T'ief? It just pass here driving fast-fast with loud music and pack-up with a set'a fellas inside. A dark-skin fella driving".

'I say, "Oh Lawd! Dey t'ief de people car!" I run back down by the house. Akse Antonio, "You call de police?"

' "Zey say zey are coming very soon'a to make'a ze statement".

'Make a statement! De car just pass through Prospect, dey could'a ketch it in Scarbro. I call de police again. "Yes, Mista Offica", I say, "is de same house. But de car just gone up de road! It now gone! Allyou could ketch it in Scarbro, I sure is Scarbro it gone. Yes, is Mista Johns'n own. Peeta Johns'n. No, he not here. You *have* to make de statement now?"

'Antonio stand up there wondering. I was sure is Scarbro de car going. Then I realise, Christ in 'eavens, dey will try and take it on de boat to Trinidad! I say I going in town to see if I could try and stop dem putting it on de boat and I hustle meself to Scarbro. When I reach, de port all light up, the back'a the big boat skin-open. I trying to explain de situation to de Customs offica: "A blue car. A Toyota Espace PPB 7420. You ain' see no car so? If you see it – it t'ief. But Jesus Christ! Look, de car coming down de road now!" It speeding coming down Milford Road and swing de corner by KFC. People pack-up inside. I run out to the road but it rev away.

'When I reach back in the house, Antonio was wit' two police offica in de kitchen. "I *now* see de car driving in town, Offica!"

'Hear them: "De same vehicle?"

' "Yes! Dat is what I was telling allyou, if you had come earlier, you could'a ketch dem".

' "Dem?"

' "Yes!" I had was to say. "De car was pack-up wit' people. Akse de lady down de road. I warn dem Customs offica a'ready on de port not to make it reach on de boat. Dey looking out fuh it."

' "Well", they say, "we can't just go driving round Tobago looking for a car just so, yuh-know. Have to take a statement . . . and then, it could go anywhere. When de Mista Johns'n coming back?"

' "Next week", I tell dem.

' "Hunf. We need a statement from de owner'a de vehicle".

' "But he not here!"

' "Well. We have some details here but when you talk to de owner, tell he to call us soon as he get back". De officas get up, pick up they hats then turn and say, "And if de car ain' reach back by the morning, call us".

' "What?" I ain' hear right.

' "If de vehicle still missing in de morning, call".

' "But . . . eh!" I shut de gate behind dem. What b'Jesus wrong wit' dese police, eh?

'Antonio was laughing.

' "You laughing! Who ever hear'a somebody t'iefing a car and then bringing it back? I don' even know people does t'ief car in Tobago! Trinidad yes, dey does t'ief car plenty. But nobody ain' go bring it back in de mornin'!" '

Thomas sat down heavy like the whole thing just happened again.

'Girl Bella, dat is how it happen, eh. And if you know how I feel to call allyou and tell you the car get t'ief. On the phone! Is only when you akse how they t'ief it, if the key still in de kitchen drawer – dat's when I realise, must be Cliff! Nobody else could'a know the key there. Cliff take it! Is madness!'

Shock nor madness, even crazy wasn't fitting. How could he do that? Why? Same time I could see the shine of the car in his eye. Betrayed 'cause he couldn't ask – snatching as if from strangers. Glad he didn't crash himself, speeding out of control. And why he didn't think about what would happen? Angry at him being so stupid, us being away, the police now involved. A stinging slap in the face and can't show tears. Can't even look at the hand that did it.

But relief. Thomas and me so glad that he brought it back.

'A joyride! De boy take a borrow! When I walk outside

and see de car there in the morning, I say, "Wait. Is dream, I dreaming!" Park back neat neat yuh-know, not a scratch. I say, "Dis fella crazy?" He think nobody go notice de car driving off *seven a'clock* in de evening?' Thomas still going on. 'I say de police know what they saying 'bout "if it not back by morning . . ." I never!'

Police had come to take fingerprints the morning the car was returned. Thomas said about four of them, with a camera, taking pictures of the car and all. Messed it up with black and white powder all over the windows and inside. He vexed 'bout how they come and do that after it was returned so neat and tidy. Cleaned it out twice still steupsing to himself, 'b'Jesus-ing'.

* * *

Sergeant Roberts and another officer coming to 'make a statement' now we're back home. All of us still wondering, figuring, trying to reason. They arrived at the gate.

'Mornin'. Mornin'. Mista Peeta Johns'n?'

'Yes, come right in.'

'You know we have to take a statement from you, the owner'a the vehicle, right?'

'Oh, yes. But it was reported that the vehicle was returned . . .'

'Yes. I was one'a them that came the next morning to investigate the case.'

Thomas cut-eye at the one responsible for the finger-print mess. Was the same Sergeant Roberts that Peter had spoken to on the phone. His manner and language surprising, pleasant, intelligent and courteous. I kept my eye on the one next to him inspecting the kitchen and staring-down the rest of the house. I slouched, folded my arms across my chest, watching him.

'We need a statement so we could get a warrant.'

'What?'

'A warrant for Cliff Dunstan's arrest. How do you know this young man?'

Peter and I looked at each other now, fears flying. 'He's an acquaintance, a friend. We met him and his brother in Plymouth, they seemed like reasonable young people.'

The other officer looked at me sly, lecherous. 'A friend?'

'Yes. Just because they're from Plymouth . . .' I stopped answering him. Thomas, too, saw the horner-woman look he gave me. Wasn't no use.

'Yes, a friend.' Peter ignored the officer strolling around the kitchen.

'Mister Johns'n, maybe you don't know what else this boy done. This is not the first time we're after him. I so happen to be the same officer on duty when the man ketch him wearing the t-shirt he t'iefed.'

'Thief? He told us about the t-shirt a few weeks ago. But he said he'd bought a stolen t-shirt.'

'Ha! He say he buy it?' Officer Lech put in. 'Well he should'a buy it wit' some'a the money he had in he pocket!'

Roberts continued, 'He t'ief a man t-shirt off his clothes line in Mount Pleasant right there, and so stupid, was walking around wearing it on the road. The man himself picked him up by offering him a ride. When he brought him into the station, the boy had almost a thousand dollars in he pocket.'

From Thomas to me to Peter, the message bounced. A frightened bird trapped in the air between us.

'What a fella like him doing with a thousand dollars?

He couldn't account for it properly. Said something 'bout some girlfriend in America send it for him! But this is not the first time we question him you-know. And now the car. He was still going to court for the t-shirt case when he come and do this.'

I saw the lash of disappointment on Peter's face before it reached me. My heart, my lips, myself stunned, crashed into glass, panic silenced. Officer Lech satisfied.

'We went to Plymuth to look for him, to his home. All the neighbours round there fed-up with him. They say they tired'a he t'iefing things from them. Sister say he does t'ief too, small things. But not the other brother.'

'Listen, that money, that thousand dollars, was stolen from here . . .' Me and Thomas stared at Peter forming it into words. 'Must be! It was he that came in here and took the money that went missing! I . . .'

Piecing together, asking questions, filling in the two-sided picture.

Roberts making notes. 'You didn't report that? He knows the house well? And the dog?'

Fools deceived. Justice raising its two-faced head. Even Officer Lech acknowledging mistakes can be made.

'But this boy have no sense! How could he think he could get away with this? We *will* ketch him. And you know there was a break-in two weeks ago in this area and another one just round the corner from here last night?' Roberts raised both hands in the air, fending off Peter's accusing look. 'We have no evidence to say is him, if it's a group a'them or what. But the lady that made the report last night saw the person run and jump down from the roof. He was very quick but it was too dark.' Got up to leave. 'We just can't have these kind'a fellas running round doing what they want to people,' waved his hand at the bright open house, 'breaking in, t'iefing. You don't know what these fellas might do next eh?'

'Um. Yes. No. I quite agree. We had no idea.' We crunched out to the gate with the policemen, Officer Lech still admiring the different angles of the house.

'I mean, this is not break-and-entry and he brought back the car, but still . . .'

They left, driving off up the road with us left looking at the car. Walked back to the kitchen, the drawer where the key was kept, right there, closed but not safe any more. The study where the money was that night, with SC sleeping in the next room, her door open. Not a shadow in the white corridor now, only us. We the shadows with shapeless feelings haunting us all around the place. Shifting shapeless feelings scudding round in me. Scrambled up, scrunched up in a knot. Cliff's hands resting on the table, his mind far away. How long he'd grown like that? Hiding himself in his body. Hiding from who, what broke him, scattered him so? Changed the balance of his blood.

Dead time and floating scum lapping at him, nudging, gently pushing. Raising dark tides in him. Dragging my body and feet in its wake.

T'ief

'CLIFF!' Was a roar from Peter's belly, so deep the name almost unrecognisable. Ripping down the night corridor towards a silhouette bent over the kitchen drawer. Pulled me out of bed, a flash of light on Peter's naked chest charging at the frozen figure holding the torch.

'What the FUCK . . .' a scramble, dash, gravel flying, Peter slamming open the kitchen door.

'Is not Cliff! Is not Cliff!' Cliff's voice screeching behind him as he pitched himself over the wall and gone. So quick, he reached the top of the road before Peter could open the gate and reach the car. My heart pounding fast as Cliff's feet.

'What? What happen? T'ief?' Oliver was up.

Thomas up too. Coming back in from the gate, cutlass in hand. 'He gone. He so quick!'

'Who? The t'ief? Cliff? Cliff?' Oliver wide awake, next to me. Peter wrapping himself in a towel. Me shaking.

'I *almost* got him, he stood right there, right where you're standing.'

Cliff's fear was in me, shocked down to my feet. The second drawer open.

'He came to t'ief the car again?'

Nobody t'iefed anything, Peter told Oliver, nothing to worry about, it's three in the morning, he should go back to bed.

'I can't believe dis boy, yuh-know!' Thomas puffed. 'Is de keys he came looking for?'

'But who is the t'ief? Cliff?' Oliver persisted.

'We don't know Oliver, go back to bed.' Peter shook his head. Couldn't believe it either. The rage that had bellowed out of him so, still showed in his shoulders and hands. My anger now growing. With the police looking for him, Cliff had the face to come so close? And then to be so stupid to be looking for the car keys . . .

'In the same place?' I said out loud. 'He looking for the keys in the same place? Like we'd be keeping them there for him?'

Thomas went and checked the basket where we now kept keys and purse. 'Is still there.'

'What's wrong with him? He thinks he so smart he could come and take the car again *when the police are out looking for him*? What else he came for? What is he after?'

I checked to see that Oliver was asleep. Stayed standing by his door.

Thomas was looking around, turning on lights. Came up the corridor from the spare room. 'This, on the bed.'

A clean towel and a pair of Peter's shorts.

'I ca—!'

The shorts came from the cupboard in our bathroom, he must have been wandering round the house.

'What was in his head? He was going to take a shower?'

Thomas chuffed. 'He was going to take a shower before he go for a drive! Huh. Maybe he was collecting them to take, they was folded up neat 'pon de bed. Nothing missing though.'

But I had told Cliff, 'I'll put a towel and some clothes

on the spare bed for you'. That night when I saw his blood change.

Thomas's face as disturbed as Peter's.

* * *

In bed, far from sleep, reasoning an answer. Trying to prove what? To which friends? Drugs? Schizo – shouting, 'Is not Cliff!'? Living 'the flim-style life' now? Police cars chasing, you racing but you smarter than them and you faster than them and fearless. Black and brave and ain't fraid'a nothing. Ready to live on the edge, or die. Or just stupid. Or confused. Like me now, trying to figure it out. Friendship to fear.

As Peter dozed I lay on his arm and my eyes kept creeping to the open doors – to see a shadow pull away quickly. The 'black dallie' standing there silent, his eyes looking away. Afraid of a friend we didn't know. He'd slid around in the darkened black-and-white house. Through the chequered lattice shadows on the floor, silent past our door, a heel and arm disappearing round a corner. But in the next room – my child sleeping – he was in there. Standing by the bed. Peering through the mosquito net. A lash jerked through me like the scream that tore me out of bed. Would Peter have hit him? He wouldn't hurt us though. Hoped I knew that. Wanting to see his face now – a chance. Where is he now – running through some black bush? Or with some friends, them asking him 'wha' happen'? laughing at him scared shit and hunted-looking. On the run since he took the car last week. Guilty. Us.

Watch Me Nuh

Sun can't smite me nor the moon by night. Bush can't hide me but not a dog could find me. Them li'l boys think was joke I joking, didn't think I could'a drive. See me speeding flying. Silva bullet. Watch me nuh. Reverse, brakes, action. Tupac rapping in yuh fucking face, a short-man stand up over fire in black and white – 'Top of the world, Ma!' Fuck chill. You ain' shit, I ain' shit, yuh mudda ain' shit. Fat-boy crying. Red Juice in me hands, steering the wheel. Not a siren behind me, a flashing blue light, a snout of a gun. Watch me nuh.

Dem couldn'a stop me. Yeah boy. All now, I could travel by road, stay by me cousin but them white cops with rifles and hounds chasing me through swamp. Wading, up to me waist in black water, alligator sliding, fear close-up in me face. Near to the ending, I now start running. Not running, walking, trekking. Under them trees by the sea-edge, a stone is my seat and branches my roof. Tracks and traces I know since a child. From Plymuth past Les Coteaux, bussing out at Culloden. Sea on me left and hills behind me, I know where the pommerac tree bearing, where whelks hiding, where cashew fruits rottening on the ground, in the tight shady valley. Silk-cotton jumbies darker than me. Spirit water, black candles and six eggs. I just a Mystic-man. Man of the past and I living in the present, walking in the future. Just a Mystic-man.

God will protec' me and the sea will cover me. Hear it getting-on down below on the rocks. Quaking the whole hillside, feel it in me feet. Raging a storm, calling in the night. Mosquitoes start feeding on blood and fruits, buzzing the darkness, frogs screeching the last light away. Sea still there, beating boo-doom. Boo-doom, boo-doom, ssshh, boo-doom. Stompy thunder-steps on the jetty, shaking it, plunking heself in the boat. Ssshh, boo-doom.

Police checking Stompy, he ain' go tell them nuthing. Pass through Plymuth, them police, cruising slow, stop by the shop, akse Masta Barbar. Can't see shit 'pon he face. Tomo go be flapping he mouth, fanning he arse in front'a them, with he fellas. The corner where them li'l boys does lime, empty. Ossi inside. Lynette must'e sorry now she talk to them police. Mudda eyes red, she ain' care what people say 'bout how 'it must would'a end up so'. Spite'a all the bush-bath she give me, pundit she carry me by, saying how something does 'take' me. She eye red now.

Peeta and Bella in they clean house. I eating dinner with them. Knife and fork shining under table lamp, black night outside and the li'l boy laughing. 'We go watch a movie tomorrow, right?' From under the giant saman tree, watch Bella bathing, washing sheself, orange bathroom light wet on she skin, black leaves moving in front me face. In she bedroom, the black dallie watching. Me in the living room falling asleep on the white settee. She come, touch me arm gentle, tell me go to me bed. Peeta done sleeping a'ready.

Jump the wall, the dog sleeping, a guard by the door, lift up he head. Gravel-scratch run! Man nor beast could catch me. Leave dem people sleeping in they house, Cliff sleeping in he bed. The lights'a Culloden breaking through ahead. From there I walking on the road to reach Scuzzy house.

*   *   *

I stay by Scuzzy a few days before we go out in he car. Next thing you know, police spot us. Like they was now coming to look for me. Scuzzy ratchafie car scrapsing round the corner, police van brakesing. He tough'n face, scar-up hands hold on tight, I gripping the door and the dashboard. Striping road walls and Moriah hills dropping straight down, small house and shops holding on tight to the road, like we. Top'a the ridge zigzagging 'cross the sky. Choking and coughing, the old car juckin'. How much'a times Scuzzy get ketch never stop he, he killing the car, mashing he foot down hard. Another corner roundsing, fencing and railings clear in front'a hilltops in the sky. Bucking, de car bucking. 'Scuzzy, we dead! We dead!' Swing in a side road and fast as we scramble out, a lightning split me head. Baton lash cracking, hands hold me, ketch me. Crunch 'gainst a banana tree, foot slipping on dry leaf. More police trashing Scuzzy, rolling like a mongoose on the ground. Back lash, kick, wood pelting pain. A blood-bawl scatter – come from my mouth? Hands slipping on soft trunk, ripping, wet flesh.

'You bawling? Loose!'

Snap me, cold iron. Wring and twist, faces, van doors ram closed, I land on a mash-up body, head hitting metal.

'Fucking bawling now!'

Banging in every pothole, slime and snivel drawl 'cross me cheek, down me neck.

'Shu' yuh mouth, boy!'

'Get out. Heh!'

'You want to play big man? Heh. Feel dis. Feel fucking dis!'

Dingy cream walls in the station.

'Aye! Wha' allyou ketch there? Magger like a one! Whe' you ketch he? Like he give yuh a fight, boy.'

'Fight? He holler like a dog.'

A big waist and a belt.

'You go see what dog does do, wait till you reach inside'a there. Oye!'

Boots stamping, the one writing in the book laughing too. 'Sign here.'

'Yuh li'l black fucking dog. T'ink you can run? Yuh friend like it in dere, yuh-know. He 'custom take blows, you ain' see he didn' leggo a sound? Tek it like a man! He 'self go make you man inside'a there. Heah. Fix yuh fucking li'l arse!'

Hands bigger than me legs, lifting, throw me down on concrete.

M u d d a

'Mudda' arrived at the door, eyes wild and roving.

'I is Cliff mudda. Un-huh. I rememba you from Sunday School. Rememba?'

Eyes met mine brief then moved on, up the corridor, glancing into the living room. She looked different from the figure I'd seen in Paris Rumshop. Young and old together. Slinky in that darkness in a tight, Chinese dress. The sheen of fabric stretched 'cross her high bumsey and small bust, the silhouette twists of hair, had melted into the dark crowd after a brief hello. Her voice now the same, deep and husky, slightly hoarse. And the same quick flash of a smile with a glint of gold.

She sat down and stuffed a purse wrapped in a plastic bag into her bra. Comfortable in her young-girl outfit: gun-mouth stretch jeans with fake frayed patches all down the legs, a bubbly Lycra vest pinched up under her breasts. Fiddling with the safety pin straining at the top of her zip, checked her worn fingernails.

'T'anks.'

She swiped the top of the Carib bottle professionally, hand going on to wipe off on her leg, eyes roving again.

'Oh Lawd, Peeta! Is Peeta right? And Bella?'

I nodded. I still didn't know what to say to her.

'Oh Gawd, I just come from de station.' Took a swig and sucked in her mouth.

She looked just like Cliff. Moved and drank like him.

'Peeta, I ain' see him yet. Dey ain' letting me see me boy!'

'The police won't let you see him?'

'No! Dey don' let me see him. Don' mind how I beg. I been there since morning, and dey ain' giving me no reason. Is beat, dey beat he!'

Wiped her face with a hand, wringing it sideways like Cliff. She had the same slightly turned-up nose and pursy lips, strong chin and round jaw muscles. Creases on her dark forehead and bags under her eyes, missing-tooth gaps in her mouth made her older. Mash-up as my insides, twisted up and tied. Cupped her forehead in her palm, bracing on the table.

'Is beat, dey beat he bad.'

'They beat him?'

'Dey beat him. Dey beat him . . .'

Hand moving to the slight goitre on her throat, her voice trembled and broke. Broke the knot in me and brought fresh worry on Peter's face.

'Since Thursday dey hold him. He an' another fella. And I hear how dey beat dem. And up to now dey still don' let me see he! I bring food, I try everyt'ing but dey not taking me on. I don' mind what else dey do but dey have no right to beat he!'

'No. They have no right to beat him,' Peter said.

She looked at him and sniffed, wiped her nose upward with the heel of her hand.

'Wha' you can do?'

For all our knowledge we still couldn't see a way. As powerless as her.

'When they caught him, Thursday?'

She swigged again. 'Yeah, un-hunh, dey hold he in Moriah. He and the fella. Dey hold dem and beat dem bad bad. People say, if you see kicks and blows. Blows! Yeah boy.'

Said it just like him.

'You t'ink is right? Gawd.'

'No, but let me try and get this straight . . .'

'Un-hunh, yes Peeta.'

'They arrested him on Thursday in Moriah and took him to the police station there. Where is he now?'

'Dey have him in town. But dey ain' bring he in de court yet cause dey beat him! Dey beat he so bad – dey don' want people to see. Oh Gawd! Is my son and dey . . .'

Skin as mine. A woman's son.

'What are they saying, why they won't let you see him?'

'Dey say de offica who handling de case not dere when I go. And dey say he ain' go get no bail, is four charge dey bringing fuh he . . . oh . . .'

'I'm sure it's because they beat him up.'

Cliff's features sitting there in his mother's face. She started picking at the label. Me gathering shreds, a mad-woman in a dry cane field, running, ripping.

'We'll do as much as we can to help but there's only so much we can do.'

'Un-hunh. Yeah boy.'

'You understand our position? First the car report was made, we weren't here . . .'

'I know.'

'. . . Then he came back into the house.'

'Yeah, I was in Trinidad when me daughter, Lynette, call and tell me de police looking fuh Cliff. First time. Oh Gawd, first time dis ever happen. And I come over from Trinidad, I was going to bring him to see you. I tell him, "Come and tell de people sorry". He uses to tell me how allyou is nice people. Treat he so nice. Anything, Ossi say, anything dey want to eat and drink, allyou always giving dem.'

Hands fluttered down, rubbing and pressing her fake patches.

'There's not much we can do now the police have him. Even before now, not until they take him to court. Once a report is made, you can't say it didn't happen. And what are the other charges?'

The rubbing agitated till she was patting her knees.

'But dey beating he . . .' voice cracked and failed.

I looked away. 'How . . .'

Peter pursing up his mouth, looking at his bare feet. Cowboy justice and lawlessness. Crime and punishment in the royal force.

'What about his uncle in the force?'

'Eh? He ain' go help he, nuh.'

She didn't want to say why. Didn't want to ask us any questions. And all the beating up in me, the racking and turning – how much she knew? The stupidness of what could've been avoided, fanning a wild rage.

'Mrs Dunstan, do you know what happened? What your son did?'

'Cliff tell me.' Twisted her face sideways to look at her heel. 'I akse him what happen, if allyou had a falling-out. He tell me no, allyou ain' do him nuthing.'

'He told you how he took the car, how after that he came creeping in here three o'clock in the morning looking for something *again*?!' Burning a scar.

'I caught him right here . . .' Peter pointed, '. . . three o'clock in the morning. With a torch, going through this drawer.'

All the pieces of flying trash, deceit and pretence while smiling shy. Damn-fool romantic me. 'He told you how much money he t'ief from us? He didn't get anything that time, but he took a *thousand* dollars from my purse before this. That's not reported or else it would be another charge! At the time we had no reason to suspect him. But now the story's out, we know other people have seen him driving the car on other occasions! He's taken the car before, it's just that this time he got caught. He tried to get into the house again – after we put the security guard on! And Lynette told the police that he t'iefs, the neighbours too?'

She'd got the label off the bottle and stuck it back on. Wiped her jeans again.

'Is like he can't help heself. Something does just take him Bella, and make him do things. Just take him so . . .' grabbed a handful of vest between her breasts, '. . . so,' twisted her fist round, 'and make him do things. Fuh no reason. And when he doing it he don' know what he doing! Yeah boy. Is somebody put a thing on he. Since he was a small boy. Something does hold him. Yuh-know is how much baptise, he get baptise? Bush-bath, all kind'a t'ing I do. And then he does be awright for a while. Then de t'ing does just come back. Somet'ing wrong with dat boy, Lawd. Somet'ing wrong with Cliff. Lynette self try how much she try. He need help. Everybody say, "He look so quiet". He does never cuss and carry on, eh. But since he small, a pundit watch he and say, "Dis boy go give you grief. Dis one here, will make you reach court. He will reach in jail". And is true! All de neighbours tell me dat bound to happen, no matter how I try. I give dat boy everyt'ing. And is so he have to turn round and get on? I don' know what to do again. But is first time he reach so far.'

'Miss Dunstan, honest, Cliff ever take drugs?'

'No! No! He never! I akse he. And I know he never take it, 'cause he have a bad chest. He can't even drink, he chest weak. It does make him sick if he take dem things. But de police never did like he. When he was working at Pigeon Point, dey always have it fuh he. Make him strip naked, search he. He alone, nobody else. Strip he naked in front'a people right dere.'

'For drugs?'

'Un-hunh, but dey never find none. Harassing he. Dat's why he stop working at de dive shop. He say he uses to feel shame in front'a all dem people. I tell he is dat picky-picky hairstyle, but he don' listen.'

'Who was he liming with?'

'Eh-heh, is bad company. I always tell Cliff an' Ossi dat. I say friends go get you in trouble. Stay home.'

'When he came back again, when the security guard almost caught him – there was a car waiting for him at the top of the road. That's the friend he was with in Moriah?'

'I ain' know nuh.'

Me asking detective questions, tracking a stranger, now in a mesh trap. And when I look in – it's no longer a stranger – my own son, writhing in pain.

She didn't look at me. Mash-up and weary.

'If you had see Cliff when he was a small boy. He and Ossi. Everybody did like dem. And he was de one dey like best. He like chi'ren, always looking out for de small ones in de yard. Not like Ossi. As he grow, he start getting in trouble. Trouble come and find he, follow he. De grandparents say they not looking after he no more. They say send Ossi but not he. Well, I keep de both'a them. Then in school, de teachers start complaining. I change schools, but still. I try, I try eh. And sometimes he moving nice-

nice with me. And then, eh, de t'ings he does do to me –
like he have no feelings. No love fuh he mudda. Dem
othas does never give me worries like Cliff. Lynette always
complaining to me. She is de one who really mind dem,
used to beat he to go to school. When she ketch he t'iefing
money she take a ten-cent and burn he hand wit' it. It
neva stop he, nuh. I tell she, he have a mind for heself
and you can never know what really going on wit' him –
all the time he looking quiet. But he neva t'ief from me.
He do t'ing, eh. But he is not a t'ief. Uh.'

'His father never bothered with him?'

'I never sit down and wait for no man to give me
nuthing yuh-know. Everyt'ing I have – is me put it dere. I
work hard to feed dem chi'ren. Me one. I tell dem stay in
de house, I don' want dem mixing with bad company.
Stay inside. Watch TV. Lynette say, dat ain' go keep dem,
she can't stop dem. But it have no work for dem these
days. Cliff need somebody to follow. When he was with
Stompy, de fisherman, Stompy use to have him by he side
everywhere he go. He uses to come and call him and keep
him here, right here . . .' crooked her arm like a wing. 'He
need a man.' Looked at Peter direct. 'Cliff like you a lot.
He talk plenty 'bout you. Come to admire and respec'
you.'

'Some kind of respect! Cliff's twenty, he's not a little
boy any more.'

'Is a man Cliff need to follow. Is only sometimes he
so.' Her bottom lip started trembling. 'Bella girl, Ossi say
he so shame. Dat's why he don' come wit' me. He so
shameface, he can't come here. And Lynette vex with me,
she say if I did talk to you before – dis would'a neva
happen. Tell allyou 'bout he ways. Maybe you could'a
have a lickle guidance on he.'

We all looked at the cat sleeping in the basket near the door. Guidance lead me where I should have known. Peter and I should've seen clear through his skin to the green in him. And through his cool and talk and moves. I should've looked through the eye-slits of his mask, touched the rough inside, smelt his breath still damp on it. How many times his shell sat here with us while he showed off outside? Lead me. Reality chasing him through pitch-black. He chasing day away. Who could've stopped him? Who could've known which way he's turning? How to hold him. How to run through old ways to new, to foreign and back, without getting caught. Get off free with fire in his head or to run again. Where? Who could've stopped you?

A Breeding in You

Is a box they put me in. A old fort. Stone block walls all round. Four fellas and me. Waiting for case to call. The walls only watching we and the blocks theyself sweating, rolling off they old paint. Grey at the bottom, mildew and cream on top. Rough old stone blocks, sweating. The skin'a the stone harden, tougher than Plymuth Point rocks, stronger than the concrete floor. Is them long-time soldiers sufferation in this old barracks. Yawsy, yellow-fever soldiers from foreign. From Peeta land? Her Majesty Royal Gaol. Stone blocks gash-up with blade saw marks, purging theyself still. Is only them alone know how they reach up here, quite up on the crown'a Scarbro hill. Plenty slave-man must'e dead hauling them up. Cold-sweat purging, wringing out 'e bad-blood. Scorning we – now we come to bring more stink and sorrow waters. Black Jay's disinfectant like a medicine in a sickroom. Waiting for case to call.

And when it call, it go have to call again: 'Come back on de fourteenth'a . . .' But you never know. Star-boy, 'I don' know nuthing' . . . I see the fella when we go outside to bathe. The thing in he eye reco'nise me but he don't want it to, watching me and them fresh convic's bathing out'a door. He ain' the only hunter inside'a here. But the coolest still. Other fellas like beasts, watching, waiting for the police scraps. In the yard, they playing like they ain' looking but they setting. From the bars downstairs, hands

waiting, to the upstairs corridor windows, eyes you can't
see, tracking you. Scraps. Is scraps I feel like too. Beat-up
hand-me-down police scraps. How you does feel when the
swelling gone down from a bruise – a shadow'a real pain
left in you flesh. Does weaken you bones. Poor-me-one
magger dog with bare ribs showing, bathing there. Trying
to wash the smell away. The water have it, the soap have
it. And now, as the breeze drop and the whole sky stop,
is the walls'a the yard have it, breathing it out. The stone
stink-breath henging in you nose. Wet, heavy rain-go-
come air. Every chest full you draw in – not enough. You
let it out – it make you tired. A renk old smell, body-soak
concrete. Strong and sour as a runting tapir in wet bush.
Is a rott'ning disease breeding in you. In you skin, inside
you mouth, in you blood 'self. Can't wash away.

And out in the yard is a box too. Top open to the sky
that stop today. Close, but no rain yet, the clouds white
and flat 'gainst the blue. Showing me how the sea colour
'eself. But sky can't sail me from this pen-up hole. The
shower pipe by the wall, same as home. Is so Ossi go
be bathing now, Lynette going to wash. Is so me days go
stop. Stop like the sky henging over me. Every li'l sound
walking far. Only noise moving. Pigs qwenking from the
prison farm on the back side'a the hill. A truck struggling
up a road. Hammer knocking nails somewhere and barky
voices talking. Metal bolts. Foot dragging on concrete,
walking. Upstairs. Down the barracks corridor, walking.
Midday hotter and stiller, coming for to carry me, for the
walls to hold me. Waiting for case to call. Corridor
windows. Walking. And there – me sea setting. Glazing
same colour as the clouds, a squinting grey-blue on the
skyline, cool green by the land and a powerful lazy blue
over so. Not moving. Only the windows framing past

Scarbro hills slope-down to the sea. Matchbox town and toy cars park-up. Still. And the sea ain' stirring. No sparking, no li'l white chips. No rash'a silver jacks jumping. Cat paws ain' scratching 'e surface today. Not a current shift on 'e face. Sea stop today.